# B E S T
# WOMEN'S
# EROTICA
# 2 0 0 2

Edited by

Marcy Sheiner

CLEIS
PRESS

Published in the United States by Cleis Press Inc.,
P.O. Box 14684, San Francisco, California 94114.
Printed in the United States.
Cover design: Scott Idleman
Text design: Karen Quigg
Cleis Press logo art: Juana Alicia
First Edition.
10 9 8 7 6 5 4 3 2 1

"Emergency Room" is from Kim Addonizio's collection of stories *In the Box Called Pleasure*, reprinted with permission from Fiction Collective 2. "Shadow Child" by Cheyenne Blue was originally published on cleansheets.com. "Learning to Play Chess" by Isabelle Carruthers was originally published on cleansheets.com. "Riding the Rails" by Sacchi Green originally appeared in *Set in Stone: Butch-on-Butch Erotica*, edited by Angela Brown, Alyson Books, 2001. "The Chocolate Dream" by Susannah Indigo was originally published on cleansheets.com. "Stone, Still" by A. R. Morlan was originally published in *Sextopia: Stories of Sex and Society*, edited by Cecilia Tan, 2001, reprinted with permission of Circlet Press. "The Flight of the Elephant" by Claudia Salvatori was originally published in *In the Forbidden City: An Anthology of Erotic Fiction by Italian Women*, edited by Maria Rosa Cutrufelli, 2000, reprinted with permission of University of Chicago Press. "Reconstructing Richard" by Helen Settimana was originally published by The Erotica Readers' Association.

# B E S T
# WOMEN'S
# EROTICA
# 2 0 0 2

*For F. S.*
*Still crazy after all these years.*

# TABLE OF CONTENTS

# Introduction:
# Sex and the World

*Marcy Sheiner*

Every erotic anthology seems to take on its own unique flavor. Although the *Best Women's Erotica* series doesn't revolve around any one particular theme, each edition appears to have some sort of underlying sensibility holding it together. Whether this is due to my own selection process or to what's happening out there with writers isn't entirely clear—it's probably a combination of these factors.

In this third annual collection of the best of women's erotica, a certain consciousness seems to have invaded the sanctity of the bedroom: A strong sense of social conditions permeates these stories. Issues such as drug addiction ("Speedball"), the death penalty, crack babies and prostitution ("Promises to Keep"), war in Sarajevo ("Reconstructing Richard"), disability ("Twisted Beauty"), loss ("The Amy Special"), and the morning-after abortion pill ("Emergency Room") have seeped into these stories, affecting the sex that the authors write about. Such weighty themes create an intensity of feeling; when sex is mixed with charged situations, it can make for some of the best sex of our lives.

When women's erotica first burst on the scene, writers treated it as a playground of sorts, a fun-filled fantasyland where we could rove and romp, exploring our sexuality out loud for the first time in history. But now it seems as if the lines between fantasy and reality are beginning to blur: not that these stories are true, but they take into account the realities of the characters that inhabit them.

That reality can be brutal, as in "Promises to Keep," or it can be hilariously funny, as in "Fuck Yer Dinner." Even the latter story, though, reflects changing social mores, and leaves us wondering about the future.

Twenty years ago I never would have imagined a story in which the main character gets turned on listening to her father having sex with another man—and then sleeps with that man herself ("Greek Fever"). Nor would I have conceived of a plot revolving around a man with unusually large breasts ("Tit Man"). On the other hand, a story like "The Adam Experiment" seems as if it has always existed, so inevitable is the author's vision—a vision based on seeing what's going on in the present and projecting its result into the future.

Poignant love stories like "Learning to Play Chess" are timeless. But "Riding the Rails" could only have been written in this particular moment in history.

In short, these stories cover a wide range of situations and emotions. As someone who frets about whether we'll run out of plots—just as I worry that we'll run out of musical variations—I'm reassured about the future of women's erotica. This latest collection has made me feel that there's seemingly no limit to the ways women write about sex. Furthermore, we're beginning to see writing—in all genres—by people who've been raised more unconventionally than the so-called baby boomers: people whose parents were hippies, queers, radicals. These writers are going to tell us stories unimagined twenty years ago, or even today. I expect to be reading color-ful tales of life on communes, or among lesbian separatist communities—all manner of "alternative families"—in the very near future, and I expect some of those stories to be woven into women's erotica. What I once thought a some-what limited genre has come to embrace the totality of human experience. Because our stories are not only about sex, and because sex itself is often about more than sex, erotic writers will never run out of new and startling themes. I am humbled and awed by the quality of the work that erotic writers send me. To them I owe a debt of gratitude for keeping the genre fresh, worth collecting, worth reading, worth getting hot over. Because of them, it is just as exciting to be editing erotica today as it was fifteen years ago.

Marcy Sheiner
Emeryville, California
December 2001

# Learning to Play Chess

## *Isabelle Carruthers*

The wet hiss of tires on the street reminds us that the window was left open. We've plunged into the Ice Age. I burrow deeper under the blanket, pretending to be asleep. I know that Adam will eventually brave the cold. He groans and rolls against me, his erection announcing a triumphant return against my hip. Our breath rises and floats above us in a small cloud.

"Close the window, wench," he grumbles. I snore lightly in response but Adam isn't fooled. His tongue slides into my ear and then opportunistically into my mouth when I open it to protest. This becomes a kiss that turns into another, deeper than the one before. I fondle him beneath the blanket and he pushes his cock against my palm with a sigh.

"You cold?"

"Mmm-hmm," is all I can manage. He tugs at the tuft of fur between my legs. I push him away, mumbling about the window.

Adam bounces from the bed. His feet pad across the bare wood floor and end in a grinding scrape as the window is forced into submission. The footsteps continue in a circuit around the room as he stops to throw more wood on the fire, cursing and prodding the reluctant flames with a pyromaniac's zeal. The iron curtain rod we've been using as a fireplace poker clatters back into the corner.

He climbs back in bed, pushing the blankets and sheets to the floor, and from this I know that he wants to make love again. Adam likes to sleep under stifling layers of blankets, but he can only fuck in open space, with nothing to cover him or impede his movements. Frigid air envelops us in shocking contrast to the warm tangle of arms and legs as we come together. He settles on top of me, his weight pushing my legs wide.

"Thighs aren't meant to be apart this long," I complain, only half kidding. I'm sore from hours of bending and stretching around him, unprepared for this marathon of sex. Except for a nap and a shower, we've done nothing else since I arrived home ten hours earlier.

Adam laughs, undeterred, knowing that I won't resist for long. He maneuvers me onto my stomach and begins to rub, kneading the abused muscles of my calves and thighs. Soon this remedy becomes foreplay and his hands embark on another mission. He strokes between my legs, teasing, waiting for me to open. I do. Two fingers slip inside and continue the massage.

Adam turns me to face him and we make love, another reunion after our long separation. He enters slowly but holds back, presses deeper and then pulls away. He watches my face and wants my reaction. This is the way Adam does everything, with this deliberate intensity. Nothing escapes his notice.

I close my eyes to avoid his. I'm afraid he'll see that I'm in love. I'm afraid I'll see that he isn't.

"Tell me," he coaxes, his lips grazing my ear and cheek, moving toward my mouth. Adam knows what I want but he waits for me to say it. I wrap my legs around him and strain upward, craving more. By now my brain is unable to form words, only syllables that mean nothing until his name escapes in a whisper. It sounds like a plea but it feels like a prayer. He touches the center of me and begins to move.

"Come for me." He is relentless, whispering this refrain again and again between kisses that leave me breathless. And this is my journey into Adam, the moment when I let go and fall into a place where there is only the sound of his voice and the rhythm I move for him, when the words that he wants to hear spill from me without restraint. Later, we surround each other with sweaty limbs, motionless for long minutes, the pulse slowing inside and out. I lie still and try not to breathe, hoping he'll fall asleep inside me, the way he used to.

Adam kisses me and rolls away to light a cigarette. Our bodies no longer touch, not like before when he always kept me close against him after making love. He's staring at the ceiling, absently rubbing his chest. I think he's forgotten I'm here. This is his bed now and I'm the stranger, this apartment suddenly a place I'm only visiting.

I wonder if he's remembering some other woman who shared this space with him in my absence. I wonder if he has a guilty conscience.

I don't ask about the nights when I called him and he should have been home but wasn't. I don't ask about the woman who answered the phone once when the machine didn't pick up. There's a feeling of something unsaid between us, and it only disappears when we make love.

It occurs to me that maybe he's been screwing me just to avoid talking, to delay an inevitable confrontation. Now I feel angry. I lean down to the floor and grab the blanket, dragging it over me. This gives me an excuse to turn away from Adam, wrapping myself against the chill. I hug the far edge of the bed, punishing him for these transgressions I imagine and the awkward silence he's caused.

Meeting Adam was a weird twist of fate, one of those things that defies destiny. Just three weeks away from leaving for a teaching assignment in Germany, I was desperately looking for someone to sublet my apartment during my four-month absence. Adam, the brother of a friend's friend, was looking for a short-term lease. By coincidence, our situations somehow became a topic of conversation between these friends, and we each ended up with a phone number to call. We arranged to meet at a bar to discuss details.

Perhaps because we both knew I would soon be gone, there was no need for the flowers-and-candy seduction that most people tolerate in order to satisfy their lust. We were on an accelerated schedule. At the pub that night we spent hours talking, and arranged a date for the coming weekend, dinner at my place and then a movie.

We never made it to the movie.

The bottles of wine that I served with dinner, much of which I consumed on an empty stomach, left me with a raging libido but hopelessly numbed senses. I managed to seduce Adam despite his insistence that he would rather wait until I was sober. Finally, unable to put me off, he took me to bed where he pumped me ferociously for an hour, to no avail. Our first sexual encounter is a disaster.

But the next morning when I wake up, Adam is still here.

I'm surprised, after the fiasco of the previous night, which I recall in gory detail. He shakes me gently awake to a breakfast of aspirin and water and then tells me to go back to sleep. I wake up two hours later and find Adam dressed and reading by the window. He's already made a trip to the coffee shop for croissants and juice. I feel wonderful but disheveled, and excuse myself to take a shower. When I return, Adam is undressed and back in my bed. He looks like he's decided to stay. He asks if I'm free for the rest of the day.

"Yeah, I guess," I say. "What do you want to do?"

"You." Adam hands me a glass of orange juice as I stand there, dumbly pondering his response.

"Oh." I wonder if I should say more—say yes, say no, say fuck-me-then-and-be-on-your-way. For once, I say nothing.

"You have a chess board under your bed," he observes, strategically changing the subject. "Do you play?" I had forgotten it was there. I don't think to ask why he's been exploring under my bed.

"Only badly," I confess.

"Good. I'll teach you." Adam rummages around underneath the bed and reappears with a large slab of black and white marble and a box containing the chess pieces, each wrapped carefully in white tissue. He sets up the game at the foot of the bed and we reverse position.

"You can go first," I offer graciously.

"OK." Adam grabs the belt of my robe and yanks, and it falls open. He arranges the fabric so that my breasts and hips are exposed. I might as well be naked.

"Better," he says, moving a pawn forward. My game goes immediately to hell. I try to avoid looking at his face because I know where his eyes will be. The sheet that barely covers him does nothing to conceal his arousal.

"There's something else interesting under your bed." His tone is casual, like he's about to tell me that I have dust on my floor. A smile plays around the corners of his mouth.

"Oh?" I feign disinterest, but I'm thinking "*Uh-oh*. I know what he's found. "What would that be?"

"A vibrator."

"Oh, yeah. That." I force a careless laugh as heat stains my cheeks. "Well...that was just a gag gift that I got a couple of months ago for my birthday," I say. This is true. "I've never even used it." This isn't.

"Uh-huh." He's grinning now, and I know he's imagining me and the vibrator. I wish I could crawl under the bed. I lose all composure and make a stupid mistake not even an amateur would commit. Adam takes my queen.

"Ouch. Damn. You took my queen?" I frown, knowing I'm in big trouble without her. "I can't believe I let you do that."

"I'm sorry." He reaches out and fondles my breast with the smooth marble tip of the captured piece. My reaction is immediate and physical. Adam drags the queen down and across my stomach while he edges closer. His mouth covers my nipples, one and then the other, tugging gently with his teeth. The chess game is forgotten.

Adam touches me everywhere. His fingers slide over and inside, searching out the sensitive spots that distinguish me from the women of his past. The soft stubble of his morning beard rubs between my legs as his tongue begins a heated exploration. I become aware of an unfamiliar pressure against my thigh as the marble chess piece begins an unhurried ascent to the place where his mouth nibbles and sucks.

The two halves of my brain do not agree on what will happen next. One half thinks this is a pretty novel approach, definitely a man who can improvise. My inner-sinner is intrigued and curious.

The other half warns that this scene is about to become kinky. My inner-saint, who strongly resembles my mother, reminds me that I'm supposed to act like a lady and should not engage in such debauchery. I reluctantly agree.

My hand moves strategically between my legs, fingers splayed to shield my virtue from further encroachment. This is a wasted effort. Adam licks my hand, his tongue moving between my fingers, wordlessly urging me to give in. I do. All inhibition disappears, and I want what Adam wants.

The warmth of his mouth recedes, replaced by the shock of a cool surface that strokes and then presses between my thighs. Adam gently works the marble figurine inside me with shallow thrusts, so slowly that I involuntarily lift against his hand and the pressure of his tongue. He brings me to the edge of climax only to pull away. And then he does it again. He makes me wait until I can't wait anymore, and the queen falls to the floor, forgotten. Adam slides into me and I slide into bliss, unaware that the sound and fury of our lovemaking travels far beyond the confines of my bedroom to entertain the neighbors as they weed their garden.

By nightfall I was hopelessly infatuated with this total stranger who, in the course of a single day, had eradicated all memory of other men, proof that the best moves we make can't always be planned in advance. We were inseparable for the few days we had left. Many mornings we would linger late in bed and play chess. Our games always ended unfinished, with the chessmen tumbling to the floor while we explored new ways to move each other. He never managed to take my queen again.

But the days passed too quickly and we never made time to talk about us, or what would happen while I was away or when I came home again. And I never told him I was in love.

Adam's weight shifts in the bed as he moves closer. His fingertips draw through my hair, starting at the temple and combing slowly to the ends, pulling the length against his chest. This is what he did once when I went to bed with a headache. I assume he's about to give me one. The silence between us is heavy with the innuendo of our stilted conversations.

"There's something I need to tell you...." His fingers stop stroking my hair and slide down the bare flesh of my arm. This is it and I'm not ready.

"It doesn't matter," I hear myself say. "You don't owe me anything." I already know what he wants to confess. I already know I can't bear to listen. He's met someone else. She's slept in our bed. Maybe he's fallen in love with her. I decide on a preemptive move to save him the trouble of destroying me.

On the pretense of stoking the fire, I leave the bed, dragging the sheet around me. I grab the iron curtain rod and beat ineffectually at the flames.

"I don't need to hear this, Adam," I say. "It's not like we're involved in some deep, committed thing. You can see who you want, do what you want. It's not like we're together—not lovers, not anything."

I've never known when to shut up, and I still don't.

"I mean, I called here a couple of weeks ago and a woman answered the phone. So I know about her. I don't care. It doesn't matter."

My diatribe complete, I turn to face him. His expression is one of stunned disbelief. He gets out of bed and begins to put on his clothes. He doesn't look at me.

"No. That's not it. That's not what I was talking about." My heart falls to my feet. "I had this card game here while you were gone. Me and some of the guys, my friends. We played poker here a few times."

I don't understand what this has to do with me. I stand there staring at the back of his head, uncomprehending. My mind stumbles over all the things I've said, trying to recall. What I remember is very bad.

"I lost your guitar."

"My guitar?" My voice rises a couple of octaves, the way it does when I've had too much to drink. "My guitar? How'd you lose my guitar?" It dawns on me that this is what he wanted to tell me.

Not a woman. Just a guitar.

"I bet it and I lost. He had a straight flush. It was stupid and I'm sorry. I really am. I'm trying to get it back."

Adam is dressed now, and walks past me to the door. He still won't look at me and he stands in the doorway, with his back to me and his hands braced against the doorframe.

"I wasn't with any other women while you were gone. My

sister stayed a couple of days, that's all. She must have answered the phone when you called." His voice is thick and I can barely hear him. "I wasn't with anyone else because I didn't want to be. It mattered to me."

And he leaves, his boots beating a steady rhythm down the stairs, not pausing, not waiting for me to run after him. He's gone. I hear the door open and close and I know he won't be back. In some long-dormant area of my brain, the words to an old song begin to play and trigger an epiphany. *Love has no pride.*

I run to the window and try to open it. Hopelessly stuck. I wipe away the frost and see him getting into his car. Heedless of the sheet tangling dangerously around my legs, I dash down the stairs. He's left the apartment key on the table by the front door. I retrieve it, and my only thought is getting this key back into his hand.

Adam's car is backing out of the driveway, already swiveling into the street. Snow is falling heavily now and his headlights aren't on. I'm not sure he can even see me in the blizzard of white, draped in a sheet the same color that makes me only part of the landscape. I run into the yard and stand there, buried in snow to my knees and waving the key at him. He finally sees me and the engine dies.

I yell at him. "You forgot your key!" After endless seconds, he starts the car again and pulls back into the driveway. He opens the door and gets halfway out, one foot in the car and one foot on the concrete. He looks at me like he thinks I've gone insane. Finally he closes the door and begins to walk toward me, his boots crunching on the snow. I'm shivering and crying and turning blue. I no longer feel my toes.

"I lied, it *does* matter," I begin, blurting out all the things I should have said earlier. "I was hurt and I didn't want you to know."

He comes closer.

"I don't care about the guitar. I can't even play it. I want you. I want chess, naked in bed with you, and whole days making love." I say more that runs together in a stream of nonsense about guitars and chess and things that lurk under my bed, but at least he's listening.

He's heard everything. It's still my move.

"I love you." I hold out my hand, offering him the small silver key. Snow falls into my palm and he stares at the key as if visualizing his life with and without the key. Life, with and without me.

Finally Adam takes the key and stuffs it into his pocket before lifting me up out of the snow. My arms wrap around his neck as he stomps across the porch and into the house. His lips are warm on my frozen cheek, tasting the tears that haven't stopped yet.

"Don't cry." His voice is soft and sympathetic. He brushes the snow from my hair. "It's OK," he says.

It will be. I climb the stairs with Adam close behind until he veers suddenly away, heading back toward the door.

"I forgot something. Be right back." I stand at the door and watch as he shuffles through the snow to the trunk of his car. He returns with a large box.

"What's that?"

"Chess," he says, trudging up the stairs.

"A new chess set?"

"Yeah."

"Oh. Did we need one?"

"We needed this one." He drops the box to the bedroom floor and unlaces his boots, tossing them in front of the fireplace to dry out.

"What's so special about it?" I move toward the edge of the bed where Adam sits, unbuttoning his shirt. The box is a bothersome obstacle on the floor between us, and I step over it to get to him.

"You'll see." He flashes that wicked grin that I love.

I straddle Adam's lap and rock against him, communicating my desire. I unbutton his jeans and stroke him through the parted fabric. "Love me," I whisper against his ear.

"I do." Adam pulls the sheet away. It hangs in loose folds to the floor and his hands cover me.

"Fuck me." I bite gently at his bottom lip, no longer shy about saying what I want.

Adam eases me from his lap and onto the bed, pulling me beneath him. I watch his eyes, knowing what I'll see reflected there.

"I will," he answers, his mouth descending to mine. "But first, I'll teach you how to play chess."

# The Chocolate Dream

*Susannah Indigo*

I walked by The Chocolate Dream every day for months on my way to work and resisted entering. Oh, I stopped and looked, like everyone did. In my case it was more at the girl behind the counter than the window display. But I am a man who has mistaken lust for love one too many times in life and thought I had learned my lesson well.

In the window: tiny chocolates in the shape of Rocky Mountain skiers, chocolate-covered cherries decorated like nipples, a layered chocolate cake smothered with strawberries, a curvy cake resembling a stripper, and a rather large chocolate dildo decorated suggestively with dripping white icing. Behind the counter: long thick black curly hair, overripe breasts, a short skirt, and those over-the-knee stockings that can drive a man to school-girl fantasies. Also behind the counter: a bearded older man who appeared to be either the owner of the bakery or her father.

It was such a simple and safe routine—leave for work, read the paper on the train, walk down 15th Street, stop and stare at her thighs while pretending to lust for chocolate.

Proceed safely on through the day with fantasies as hot as Paris when it sizzles.

So you can imagine my surprise the day the dildo disappeared.

I thought perhaps I had only dreamed it all. The entire erotic display was gone. Proper little candy boxes lay open on the red doilies. A three-foot-tall wedding cake towered over them.

What could I possibly do? A man has to know why things happen. I opened the door and went in.

The stockings came toward me. "Hi, I'm Allegra, can I help you?"

Allegra? How well it fit her. Her voice was as soft as windchimes on a slow summer day. Her tiny black-and-white plaid skirt swayed in front of me like the breeze. A girl who can make you think those kinds of things is not to be taken lightly. I looked closer and could see that she was not a young girl at all, but a regular adult, like I was supposed to be.

"May I help you?" She looked a bit wary at my silence, probably having seen her share of perverts admiring the window display.

Yes, I thought. You can tell me exactly how many inches of thigh are bare between your stocking tops and your hem. Or you could just let me measure it with my hands.

Instead I muttered dumbly, "Hello. I see your dildo has disappeared."

She laughed. "Yes." She looked me up and down and I could feel her taking in my three-piece suit and my monogrammed briefcase.

"You're a lawyer?" she asked.

Man, I hate that it shows. The worst part is that it shows even when I'm in blue jeans. It's been killing me for fifteen years now. I once dreamed of being a great writer, saving the world with my journalistic exposés on the way to glory. I think I was afraid, and law school seemed a safer bet. I made up the excuse to myself that a legal education would help with my dreams. But it's difficult to save the world when you ride the train and kiss ass to rich people all day long.

"Yeah, I'm a lawyer." I wanted to take this Allegra in my arms and run off to a new life. Either that or just bend her over the bakery counter and lift her skirt and pull down her panties and kiss her from her stocking tops up to her ass.

"I have problems here," she said with a frown. It was really more of a pout.

Problems were my life. Just once I wished a client could prance into my office and tell me they needed me even though they had no problems. But problems involving pretty girls and missing chocolate dildos at least seemed interesting.

I checked my watch and made the decision that would affect the rest of my life. "Tell me what happened. A burglary?"

"Come on in the back," she replied. I followed the swaying skirt through the rear door.

"I'm Bret, by the way. Bret Dublin." She shook my hand and I never wanted to let go. "Where's your boss today?"

She lifted her cute ass up onto a desk and laughed at me. "My boss? You've watched me every day through that window and you thought he was my *boss?*"

Stupid didn't quite describe my feeling. "He's not?"

"You gotta watch those stereotypes, Bret Dublin. I own The Chocolate Dream. Zach is just an artist who does work for me. He was one of my teachers in art school."

I knew nothing. She flipped on the radio to a beautiful rendition of Sarah Vaughan moaning about "ain't misbehavin, savin' all my love for you." So I asked Allegra to dance.

I don't know what I was doing dancing this young woman around the back room of a bakery when I should have been at my desk meeting old Mrs. Carey to discuss how to safeguard all the millions from her estate, but there I was. And she was with me all the way. Fred and Ginger. Or maybe I just dreamed it.

"Tell me what you do here, Allegra." I know I was at least much closer to her, like up on her desk with my thigh pressing against her bare one while I surveyed her high-tech back office. A couple of computers in one corner and a constantly buzzing fax in the other implied a little more business going on than just wedding cakes.

"Ah, Bret, I make dreams come true. Of the chocolate variety. Most of my business is mail order—custom chocolates for any occasion."

Have I mentioned I love chocolate? Allegra was talking about chocolate dreams like they mattered, and I vaguely remembered having my own dreams once.

"Marry me, Allegra."

"What?"

"Marry me and give me back my dreams. I'll solve all your problems."

Some girls would have walked away. Allegra hugged me. And then she told me I was crazy.

"Come see the kitchen, Bret baby."

I knew I could fall deeply in lust, or even love, with a woman who would call me "baby" ten minutes after she'd met me. I put my arm around her waist and she didn't take it away. Visions of bare thighs coated in melted chocolate filled my mind as I followed her to the kitchen.

Candy molds were everywhere. Sports shapes, holiday symbols, and every erotic image possible. Dildos, cocks, nipples, pussies, couples intertwined, little handcuffs, and slinky gartered legs.

"We make everything here. I've never turned down an order. I just call Zach and he fires up the mold in his studio. People love the sexy chocolates the best. Know who the number one customer is for them?"

"No, who?"

"Republican women. I'm not making that up. I keep track with a survey of my regular customers. Republicans call them vibrators, Democrats tend to call them dildos, but they're still my number one best-seller. Both the tiny ones and the larger size."

I'd heard stranger things. Repression does wonders for sexuality. "So now tell me, Allegra, what happened?"

"It's a long story. It started when I got a letter from that 'Focus on Moral Superiority' group. You know the ones with their noses in everyone else's business? Come home with me tonight and I'll tell you the rest."

Layers of lust overtook me as I sat in Allegra's kitchen and watched her at the stove. I wrapped my arms around her waist and pressed up against her while she talked and cooked.

"So," she said, pressing back against me and letting me pour wine from my glass into her beautiful mouth. "The letter comes in one day. It says that city laws prohibit pornography businesses within 700 yards from houses, schools, or churches. We're downtown, right? And there's no churches within three blocks. But it turns out that almost empty building down on the corner with a couple of little shops upstairs used to have a small private school on the ground floor, and is still licensed for it. Now, I don't think I traffic in pornography, I traffic in food and dreams. But it scared me enough to take down the display and start worrying about the back room chocolate-toy business. They just want to shut me down."

"Hmmm, " I answered with my lips heading down to her bare neck, "You *do* need my help."

She turned and kissed me. "I do."

"But," she added, " I asked my own business lawyer and he just said that technically they're right, and I should take away all visible signs of anything anyone could consider obscene. I've never had one single complaint about my shop from anyone before this. People *love* the display."

"Why do you think I can do anything for you, Allegra?" I knew exactly what I could do for her, and I wanted to do it right there on the kitchen floor.

"Truth?"

"Of course."

"Because every day when I watched you watch me through the window, I thought you looked like a man with imagination. I always wondered who you were. And what your hands would feel like on my bare skin."

Love. This couldn't be just lust. My hands travelled quickly to her ass and cupped it and lifted her up toward me. "Turn off the stove, Allegra."

She obeyed and turned back to me and I lifted her up and wrapped her legs around my waist. I kissed her deeply and spun her around, ending up by her big black leather sofa. I whispered what I wanted while I started to unbutton her blouse. "I want to bend you over the back of this sofa, baby, lift your skirt, and spend all night travelling from your toes right up to your heart."

She kissed me softly and said, "No, Bret baby. Not yet."

I knew what she wanted. I had listened to her story about how her grandfather opened his bakery in this building in 1925, and how it was failing when Allegra took it over from her mother. This location was her life. She lived above the shop in a refurbished loft and planned to stay there forever. I stayed awake at night searching for a solution. I knew they would frown on pro bono work for dildos in my office.

Allegra made me dinner every night for a week and we talked about what she could do to fend off the "Moral Superiority." She lit candles and played soft jazz and she put her hand on my thigh during dinner and said, "I know you can figure it out."

She was a tease, this Allegra, but an honest one. The night I came up with the absurd, yet creative, idea about how to hide the erotic chocolates as religious symbols, she offered to show me what a woman could do with a chocolate dildo. She raised her skirt and leaned back against the pillows on the floor and spread her legs. I watched from the sofa above as she teased herself with a chocolate dildo that closely resembled the size of my own hard cock. When she slid the chocolate into her pussy, I felt like a teenager about to come in my pants.

"Dessert?" she offered afterward, handing me the chocolate for a bite. Chocolate had never tasted quite like that before. I don't know why she trusted me so much to control myself, but she said she could read my character, and she was right. Plus, the waiting was powerfully intense.

The night we drew up the detailed blackmail plan, she invited me to spend the night. The plan included a lengthy list of conservative right-wing women, *and* men, who had made purchases through "The Chocolate Dream," complete with addresses and credit card numbers. I still have this list somewhere, with the title "Conservatives for Pro-Chocolate." In the end it smacked up against both of our ethical standards, but she still invited me to sleep with her. No sex, but wrapping my arms around Allegra's naked body and spooning her close and whispering each other asleep still rates as one of the all-time most erotic moments of my life.

I researched every possible angle. We laughed about the law. No porn near churches? "Right," she said, "those folks are some of my best customers." But I knew she was scared about losing the whole thing.

I met with several other lawyers wise in the ways of pornography, and they said she was out of luck. The statute would never be repealed, because who wants to agree to thrust porn on innocent children or righteous churchgoers? And there were no exceptions to the statute. All the "Moral

Superiority" group had to do was subpoena her records and chart out just how much of her business came from dildos and nipples and she would be closed down.

In the meantime I was fascinated watching her orders come in. A woman in Iowa placed an order for a private fundraising party—I looked at the fax as it came in:

2 DZ  *Rep. vibrators*
4 DZ  *Dem. dildos*
3 DZ  *mini-handcuffs*
6 DZ  *white chocolate cherry nipples, individual pkgs.*
1 8" *dark chocolate dildo, ribbed*

Allegra was nonchalant about these orders; I was either on the floor with laughter or deep in erotic dreams at night picturing this secret world of chocolate kink that I had never known existed.

We considered moving the shop—the obvious answer. But to be legit, she would have to file a statement with the new community that she was in the business of selling pornography, and she refused. I couldn't blame her. She also refused to locate anywhere near the known porn strips. The truth was that the 15th Street location was her heritage, all she had left of her grandfather, and she was going to live out her dream right there, one way or the other.

The night she offered to paint my body with warm chocolate was the night I knew what I was going to do. My ethics were going to have to take a short vacation while I solved Allegra's problem. There was no way I was ever going to let her go. Ever.

She took a soft brush and made a design on my torso with warm chocolate. Then she licked it off slowly, and it was like a dream. I lay back and closed my eyes as she worked her designs down my body, one at a time, stroking and then licking. It took forever, like all good dreams do. When she reached the design on the tip of my cock and licked it all off, I fed her everything I had mixed in with the chocolate in her mouth. She was beautiful, and she was hungry for me and I wanted to feed her for the rest of my life.

I met with old, rich Mrs. Carey in my office the next morning. I told her I had the perfect, the only, the most profitable location to invest in for her idea of opening a restaurant with several trendy boutiques up above. It was easy. I told her that her grandchildren would be taken care of for life, and that they would think she was the coolest grandma on earth. I have no idea if this was true, but it seemed like a good dream to have. She authorized the check and I offered it to the school-building owner the same day. He couldn't refuse; he even snickered to me that he couldn't stand kids anyway and his own dream was to open an X-rated video store down on Colfax. Licensing paperwork was completed and filed, and the details assigned to my paralegal to finish up. I arrived triumphant at Allegra's loft at six sharp.

"Sit down, Allegra, you're not cooking tonight. We're having chocolate for dinner."

I placed the papers in her lap and let her read with delight while I got ready and talked about my plan.

"Tonight's mine, baby. And so are all your tomorrows." How I loved that she could inspire me to say things like that.

"Yes," she said softly, agreeing to everything I said.

When she returned from downstairs with all the extra available chocolate toys I asked her for, I was ready for her. I showed her the large chocolate handcuffs tied with ribbons that Zach had made for me. We both knew she could just bite her way through them, but we both knew she wouldn't. I undressed her, laid her belly-down on the bed, fastened her wrists to the brass headboard, and settled in to eat.

The taste of the inside of a woman's thighs coated with juices and chocolate is only surpassed by the joy of finally holding the ass you have dreamed of tight in your hands and discovering that lust and love can be exactly the same thing.

I placed the order with Zach this morning for the wedding chocolate forms, all quite sensual and erotic. Allegra doesn't have much time for the details of our upcoming celebration, since she's busy working on the new Chocolate Dream franchising I helped her put together. I, on the other hand, have what seems like all the time in the world, as I sit in my small office space over the shop and spend my time writing and helping Allegra with the legal end of the business. My firm was most generous when I left, and every lawyer in the place envied my escape. I sent them all their very own box of chocolates as a parting gift—little chocolate desks with little people handcuffed to them. Some of them stop by here often to visit the Dream.

# The Adam Experiment
## Renee Carter Hall

Adara looked up from her notes, casting another glance toward the subject's glass-enclosed quarters. The man was seated at his computer, working through one of the colorful logic puzzles that kept his mind occupied during most of the day. His attention seemed to be wandering, though; he was taking several minutes longer than usual to finish this one.

She recorded the observation in her notescreen's first-shift log. Detailed observation of the subject was her job, shared by three other women who alternated shifts throughout the day and night. They studied him almost as a new species: the first man to exist in countless generations.

She scanned through past records. On many occasions, restlessness had led him to masturbate. They used devices to collect semen samples from him for their experiments, but at times he resorted to this wasteful stimulation on his own impulse. None of the computer models or the engineers had predicted this.

Adara watched him stand and walk to his bed, one of the few pieces of furniture in the room. As he wore no clothing, he required little storage space. The computer provided mental stimulation, and staff members delivered his nutritionally perfect meals. A small bathroom with shower and toilet adjoined the main area. One-way glass allowed the staff to easily view his entire living space.

She walked to a vantage point near the bed. Yes—as expected, the penis was erect. She noted the manual stimulation, then waited.

It certainly seemed to be pleasurable for him—he exhibited many of the same pleasure signals observed in women. Whether he masturbated from true need or simple boredom, no one knew or even bothered to ask. It was merely something else to record.

She noted the time of ejaculation and the approximate amount of semen expelled. Many of the women were openly disgusted by his practice, and complained at having to watch and record such an event, placing it on the same level as measuring his excreted waste. She had felt the same way the first several times.

She almost felt sorry for him, though she could never have admitted it to any of her colleagues. Emotional attachment was—well, unwise. After all, for the foreseeable future at least, this was only an experimental subject.

Still, she couldn't control her feelings. And although what he did was crude by all accounts, she admired his ability to be so natural. Of course, he didn't know he was under constant watch, and he knew very little about their society or the outside. There was no need to educate him further—not at this stage, anyway.

He would probably sleep now; his vital readings were indicating the state of relaxation following orgasm. At least he could have some pleasure in his life, she thought. And yet he couldn't have that wonderful intimate peace she'd felt with her lover last night, curled breast to breast, fondling each other to climax.

The memory stirred her. She called up the message screen and dashed off a note inviting Celina to her quarters after the work cycle. She sighed a bit as she sent the message—she enjoyed Celina's company and had agreeably accepted her offer to take their relationship to a physical level; but secretly she envied the relationships so many of her colleagues had. They talked about their partners—some almost constantly—and they were pleased to be with them, to be seen with them as a couple, even as a bonded pair. She thought of all the love poems she'd read in her literature courses, all the romances she'd seen in vids and in real life. She'd never felt anything like that.

Enough. She turned back to the glass and watched him sleep. After a few minutes her gaze strayed to his penis, now lying flaccid against his scrotum. Penetration was an animal act, from the days before technology made it, and men, obsolete—but she suddenly wondered how it would feel.

She'd heard of women using devices to simulate penetration, soft rods to insert in the vagina. She'd never seen one and had no idea where others went to get them. It must be a pleasant feeling, though, or the underground fetish wouldn't exist.

It would feel warm, she decided, when he inserted his penis and when he ejaculated. It might....

The chimes startled her. The shift was over. Feeling a little dazed, she looked down at her notescreen, scribbled a few lines to finish up, then left and went to her quarters.

Celina wasn't there when she arrived, so she used the time for a quick meal and a shower, her thoughts wandering from Celina to the man, from anticipation to anxiety. In the shower, she focused the pulsing spray between her legs, wondering if his climax might feel that way. The spray was like her thoughts—strong in a way that excited and frightened her simultaneously.

"Adara?" Celina's voice outside.

Hurriedly she turned off the shower and dried herself, putting on a blue silk robe that Celina liked. Natural fabrics were expensive, but her line of work paid well enough for the occasional luxury.

They kissed. "I'm so glad you called," Celina said. "It's been such a long day. I thought I had that formula all worked out, and then I ran it through the variable tests…. How were things for you?"

She tried to think of what to say, and at last decided on, "The usual."

"Whatever that means," said Celina with a short laugh. "I know—classified. Someday I'll have to get clearance just so I can find out what it is you do all day." She pulled at the belt of Adara's robe. "At least I know what you do at night."

Adara hesitated. "What if we try something different tonight?"

"Different? What?"

She struggled to find the right words. "I've been wondering what it would feel like if you would…well…try putting your fingers"—there was no stopping now—"inside."

"*Inside?* You mean—?"

Adara nodded, heart pounding.

Celina frowned, obviously searching for a polite way to refuse. "I…I don't think I should."

Adara tried to keep the disappointment out of her voice. "I only thought—"

"Besides, I might hurt you. I don't know how you're supposed to do that…that sort of thing." She studied Adara. "You been watching blacklist vids or something?"

"No, I just…wondered," Adara finished lamely. "You're right. I'm sorry—never mind."

Slowly they began their usual erotic play, stroking and touching. Celina said nothing more about the suggestion, but Adara knew there was no going back, not even to the casual connection they'd had before. Each time Celina looked at her, she could hear the unspoken question: "Why on earth would you—would anyone—want *that?*"

She enjoyed an intense climax, as always, but was relieved when Celina finally left. Lying alone in bed, she tried to forget the entire evening; she kept hearing Celina's voice refusing her.

*And why shouldn't she refuse?* Adara thought. *What's wrong with me? I'm not the kind of woman who should want to be—to be—* She couldn't even find a word that suited the act she craved, the fantasies that teased her with the hope of something more, a connection beyond the physical, a love that would deny her nothing.

She slept deeply, and upon awakening the next morning had the disturbing sense that she had dreamt about him. She couldn't remember any details, but the feeling stayed with her as she dressed and went to work, absently skimming the previous shift's observational notes.

Probably it was all just stress. And the usual hormones would be playing a part, too—she was scheduled for her procedure in just another week, when her eggs would be harvested to engineer more female embryos. She'd find a new lover eventually, someone who would indulge her. Beneath that thought, though, was the nagging feeling that it would always be hollow, that something else, something she couldn't even name, would still be missing.

He had eaten breakfast, she recorded, and the remnants of the meal had been removed. He was now attending to matters of personal hygiene. She recorded the time at which he stepped into his shower, the time at which he stepped out; she was still preoccupied, calling up the message screen to write to Celina, wondering whether to say it straight out or ask to meet, to end it face-to-face.

A warning flashed on her notescreen. Alarmed, she scanned the text, then realized what she'd done. The glass that separated him from her was usually opaque to him and transparent to her. But somehow she'd accidentally disabled it—and it was transparent both ways.

Maybe he hadn't noticed, maybe she could get it back up before—

She glanced up. He was looking back at her.

She blushed, not because she wore only the customary wrap around her waist, but because of her job—to watch him, unnoticed. She felt as if she'd been caught spying.

All this time, she'd watched him, observed him, and yet— how could it be?—she'd never actually *looked* at him. And he was beautiful. His hair was a deep, rich shade of brown that framed his light green eyes and softened his features. His eyes were incredibly expressive—right now they showed a mixture of surprise, alarm, and fascination. She figured her own expression looked the same.

He was in perfect condition—she knew that from the reports, but now she saw it as well: how his muscles worked smoothly in tandem as he approached the glass, how his physical presence radiated strength, health, and unashamed sensuality. Within her, desire uncurled and responded.

But Celina was healthy and beautiful, too, just as her other lovers had been, and she'd never felt this.

Maybe it was simply because he was different. Anything exotic is erotic, she reminded herself. And he was certainly exotic.

But this was more than carnal attraction; it was something that caught her breath and held it, something that satisfied unknown needs, that invited and welcomed, beckoned and promised. Was this what so many of her colleagues felt, what so many of the women had with each other, what she thought she was abnormal for never feeling?

One thing, at least, was certain: She wasn't going to accept this glass any longer. And so, while every part of her shrieked that this was the end of her career, the end of everything, she punched in the emergency code, unlocked his doors, and went inside.

*Why shouldn't I go to him?* she thought, amazed by her own defiance. *We're the only ones who can really understand each other. I know how it is to be alone in the midst of so many.*

He backed away when she entered. Understandable. He'd seen the women before, of course, on their usual rounds, at set times each day. She'd disrupted his routine. They'd all been warned that disrupting the schedule would cause stress, and stress could interfere with his health, and now she was breaking that rule and who knew how many others; more important, she didn't care.

"It's all right," she said, conscious of the tension in her voice. "It's all right."

What could she do to comfort him? She decided to try what soothed her most.

She touched his arm gently, lightly, and when he didn't recoil, she touched his chest—so flat, she marveled, so smooth in that way; the short wiry hairs were fascinating to touch. She stroked her hands along his body and led him to the bed so that they could sit down.

He seemed much more relaxed now, and she felt pleased with herself that she had thought of such an effective solution. No, it was more than that: She was glad to see him content.

Then he began to touch her, lingering over her breasts, along her back. She started to protest, then stopped. Naturally he was curious; why not provide the means for him to question and discover?

She sat up a bit, tilted her head, and kissed him slowly. After a hesitant moment, he returned the kiss, then kissed her shoulders, her breasts. She reminded herself that the mouth and lips were far more sensitive than the fingers, far better for this type of exploration—and then he brushed his fingers over the fabric that covered her.

Well, she thought idly, it wasn't fair that she should be clothed while he was naked—so she stood and unwrapped the cloth from her waist, letting it fall to the floor.

She returned to the bed and saw, with some surprise but not shock, that he had an erection. Her fantasies returned with a tempting rush, and she knew she wasn't satisfying just his curiosity, but her own as well.

She thought of what he did for stimulation, the way he touched his penis. She could do that for him.

She grasped the shaft gently, pulling the loose skin back toward his body. He made a quick, soft sound of pleasure, so she repeated the motion, more slowly this time, intrigued by how warm it felt, how it pulsed in her hand, so similar to her clitoris. She felt the way she did when Celina touched her, or when she touched herself: restless, feverish, yearning.

Without a second thought or even a first, she slid her other hand past her labia and began stroking her clitoris, already swollen and sensitive. When she noticed the clear droplet at the very tip of his penis, she touched it, rubbed it between her fingers, and used it to smooth her touch. Then at last—he wouldn't think it odd, he wouldn't even know it was abnormal!—she plunged two fingers into her vagina, finding it new and strange and wonderful all at once.

How could she tell him what she wanted? Soon enough she realized she didn't have to—oh, instinct was a marvelous thing, knowledge from deep inside, inherited from those thousands of years ago when men and women shared the world. In this same way, she was sure, erect penis and open vagina each would find and fit the other.

She guided him inside. There was an instant's pain, enough to make her doubt her judgment, but then it was gone and there was only pleasure and rhythm encoded in their blood and breath. She rubbed her clitoris in time with his thrusting, thinking *We're doing it like animals, the way they mount and come, the way we used to, like animals, and maybe it isn't right for all of us, but oh, it's right for me, it's right and hard and soft,* and then she was coming and so was he, and she knew his semen was rushing into her, the way it spurted out when he rubbed himself, inside her now, and then she lay still and panting under him, loving him, waiting to see what would happen next.

She'd forgotten about the cameras. She remembered them a moment after, her perspiration drying on her breasts, his issue drying on her thighs.

Lazily she wondered what they would do to her when they arrived. Certainly she wouldn't have her job any longer. Maybe they had some way to induce amnesia, give her a fresh new mind and an acceptable libido. Maybe they'd kill her—in some humane way, of course. She'd rather die than forget.

The director arrived a few minutes later, entering the room as if nothing were amiss. Silently she wrote a few lines on her notescreen, then picked up the discarded wrap-cloth and took it with her.

*Of course*, Adara thought, admiring the logic of the solution. They'd studied him long enough by himself. Now, a new experiment.

She went to his terminal and tried to open the observation files. She was denied access to all but the opening page:

ADAM EXPERIMENT B: EVE VARIABLE INTRODUCTION CLASSIFIED

She didn't need to check the doors to know they would be locked. Drowsily she returned to the bed and slipped into his embrace. One day, she decided, they would leave together. Sure, the directors had changed all the codes by now, but she could break them eventually, and then they would escape to somewhere remote, some place they'd have each other and everything they'd need.

Her dreaming changed as months passed and she slowly began to understand why she couldn't keep meals down, why her body began to change, her belly and breasts swelling.

*Like animals,* she thought happily, and hoped for a boy.

# Emergency Room
## *Kim Addonizio*

He asks if I've been tied up before. I tell him yes, and he wants to know for how long. Tell me about it, he says. I feel shy; I don't want to go into details. We're sitting in Vesuvio's at four in the afternoon, drinking gin and tonics. He has his hand on my thigh. I'm madly in love with him—we've known each other three weeks. I'm not ambivalent like I usually am, everything about him seems perfect: his close-cut black hair, the way he puts his tongue down my throat when he kisses me, his blunt, square hands. He's the sexiest man I've ever been with. It scares me that I can feel so happy. None of our friends think it will last.

I want to tie you up, he says. I want to do things with you that you've never done with anyone.

A man at the bar is doing card tricks. He holds up the queen of diamonds and shows it to a pale, pretty girl in a black leather minidress, black fishnet tights, and heavy black combat boots. The girl looks bored. She glances over at us and sees me watching her. She takes a card from the magician's deck, looks at it, and sticks it back in.

We get drunk sitting in Vesuvio's. At seven o'clock we're still there, kissing passionately, his hand under my T-shirt squeezing my breast. No one pays any attention to us. The magician is still there, too, talking to another woman. He holds up the queen of hearts. Finally we get hungry and walk around the corner to Brandy Ho's and eat Kung Pao chicken and Szechuan shrimp, sitting next to each other in the red leather booth. I feel like I'm in an alternate universe. Everything looks familiar but it's different than before. The sexual intoxication is overwhelming, I can't function in the real world: I haven't called my friends, paid my bills, read a newspaper since all this started. I don't want it ever to end. I feel vulnerable and it's terrifying; I can't help being in love with him, even if he leaves me or treats me like shit I can't hold back the way I usually do, I have to give him everything. Then I won't know who I am anymore.

With his glasses on he looks like a different person: shy, slightly studious, younger. It's as if he's in disguise; I don't recognize him as the same person I fuck. I like him in his glasses, like the idea that there are things about him no one could ever guess from the way he looks. He takes his glasses off, sets them on my kitchen table.

Take off your clothes and stand against the wall, he says.

I peel off my T-shirt, drop my skirt and underwear, and lean against the wall, facing him. He tells me to put my arms above my head. We've just finished dinner. He pours himself more wine and tips his chair back, drinking the wine, watching me.

Don't move, he says. He leaves the kitchen. I hear him pissing in the bathroom. I'm excited, scared, I don't know what's going to happen next. I close my eyes, listen to the stream of piss hitting the water in the bowl. My neighbor in the next apartment starts playing the clarinet. She's just learning so it's all honks and squeaks. The walls are thin, I'm worried someone will hear us, I don't want anyone to hear us. I don't want anyone to know what we do together, what he does to me.

He comes back to the kitchen, zipping his pants. He takes an apple from the bowl of fruit on the table.

Open your mouth.

He shoves the apple against my mouth; my teeth sink into it. I'm gagged. He's not gagging me. I can drop the apple any time. I want him to dominate me, use me; I want to be his slave. I have to understand submission, why it's so erotic for me; I can't reconcile it with the rest of my life. I've never let myself physically explore how I feel because intellectually I can't accept it. Women are shit, they're only here for men's pleasure, men control everything.

My beautiful slut, he says. Look how wet you are. He puts his middle finger inside me, then in his mouth. He unbuckles his belt and takes it off in one smooth motion.

One Saturday night when we're fucking the condom breaks. I know I'm ovulating, I don't want to get pregnant. He calls a sex information hotline and asks what we can do, and they tell him there's an abortion pill I can take; I should call a doctor to prescribe it.

I call the advice line at Kaiser and get put on hold. I wait forty-five minutes, then a voice comes on the line and says there's one more call ahead of me. I wait ten more minutes. The woman on the other end tells me she can't help me, I need to talk to Doctor X. I ask her to connect me. She connects me to the wrong extension; the people there tell me to call a different number. I hang up, dial the main hospital, and ask for Doctor X.

He's not on tonight.

I explain what's happening. The woman on the other end insists that Doctor X isn't there, and no one else can prescribe the pill. Finally someone else gets on the phone and tells me that Doctor X is being paged. I'm put on hold again. A Muzak version of "We've Only Just Begun" by the Carpenters plays, followed by the Beatles' "Here, There, and Everywhere." Twenty minutes later another person gets on the line.

Can I help you?

I think I'm being helped. I don't know. I've been on the phone for an hour and a half, I'm trying to reach Doctor X.

I want to scream at the person on the phone but she is very nice, it's not her fault, there's nobody to blame, I don't want to scream at her. I don't want to have a baby. I'm thirty years old, I work at a cafe and never have enough money for art materials. My mother was a painter, she stopped after she had me. I can't be a painter if I have a baby. He doesn't want a baby either. Not this way, he says. Not by accident.

Please hold, the nice person says. I listen to a few bars of "My Cherie Amour." A minute later Doctor X gets on the line.

You have to come to the Emergency Room to pick it up, he says.

Can't you just call it in to a drugstore?

We have to see you, he says. There are certain risks involved.

He says that if the pills don't work and the fetus is female it could be turned into a boy by the hormones. Masculinized, he says. The fetus might be masculinized and if you decide to have the baby there could be problems.

I don't want to have the baby, I say. I want the pills. If they don't work I'll have an abortion, but I've had three abortions already and that's why I want the pills. Please, I say. Can't you call it in?

You have to come to the Emergency Room, he repeats, sounding annoyed. We have to have a record that we've seen you.

I hang up. It's ten P.M., we haven't had any dinner. He puts his arms around me.

He says, I hate to see you go through this.

I hate doctors, I say. I hate Western medicine. I hate Kaiser, you never see the same doctor twice. Nobody knows you or gives a shit about you, you're a name on a chart. Why can't they just give me the pills?

Let's go eat first, he says. I'll take you some place nice, we'll forget about this bullshit. The Emergency Room will be open all night.

He takes me to Little Italy. We drink a lot of wine. I start to feel better, now it's an adventure we're having together instead of a lousy experience. We joke about it, he puts his hand over mine on the red-and-white checkered tablecloth. I've never been so in love with anyone. I tell him I don't think I want any children.

I'll get sterilized, I say. I'm no good at birth control, I always blow it one time and get pregnant from that one time. I'll make an appointment and get my tube tied. I only have one tube and ovary because I had an infection once and had to have an operation. A gynecologist told me once that if I ever got sterilized it might be major surgery, because of the scar tissue from the other operation.

I'll get a vasectomy, he says. It's easier, it's just an office procedure.

What if we break up and you want to have a baby with someone else? As I say this the thought of it makes me jealous and depressed and I'm sure it will happen.

I can go to a sperm bank, then. Besides we're not going to break up. And you might change your mind. Five years from now we might want a baby and we could have one.

We get to the Emergency Room a little before midnight. We sit in the waiting room, and after half an hour a nurse leads me through a curtain and takes my blood pressure.

I'm only here to pick up a prescription, I tell her.

She ignores me, fastens a yellow plastic ID bracelet with my name and policy number around my wrist. She leads me to an examining room where there's a metal table with stirrups, and puts a blue plastic gown on the table.

Wait here, she says.

I sit down on the only chair. After forty-five minutes a Chinese medical student comes in.

I need to examine you, he says.

No, you don't. I'm not sick, I just need a prescription.

I'm supposed to examine you.

I think of him looking at me, my legs spread apart, my heels in the cold stirrups; I don't want him to look at me. I start crying and saying I just want the pills, there's nothing wrong with me I don't want a baby you don't need to examine me, please just give me the pills so I can go home.

He writes something down on his chart, then walks out, muttering something I can't hear. A minute later the nurse says I can go back to the waiting room.

A man with long blonde hair is passed out in one of the chairs. Three well-dressed black people are sitting together. The man is doubled over, holding his side, and the two women are on either side of him talking to him and rubbing his shoulders. There's a Toyota commercial on the TV, then an episode of *Miami Vice*. The nurse comes out after twenty minutes and tells me that Kaiser's pharmacy doesn't have any more of the pills; there might be some at Mount Zion, she has to call and then send someone there to pick them up.

I lean my head on his shoulder; he strokes my hair. The blonde man wakes up and looks around the room. Fuck this shit, he says. He gets up and walks out.

At three A.M. the nurse calls me in behind the curtain and hands me a paper cup of water and another paper cup with three tiny white pills in it. She gives me three more to take in twelve hours.

When we leave, the black people are still sitting there.

I have an almost pathological need for other people's approval. If someone criticizes me I fall apart, I feel useless, stupid, insignificant. When I confess this to him he says I need to learn not to internalize other people's negativity. I experience this as subtle criticism and move to the edge of the bed, away from him.

I used to sleep with men so that they would like me. I always had a lot of lovers. Now I only fuck him; he excites me more than anyone. When I masturbate I don't think about strangers fucking me, the way I used to; I think about him looping a rope through a ring screwed into the top of the doorframe, slapping my breasts and cunt. I think about the way he growls low in his throat, the violence of his orgasms. I masturbate imagining he is watching me, and come saying his name over and over. My life before I knew him seems impoverished, a desert. I'm afraid of losing him; he has to keep reassuring me that he loves me and wants me. At parties I'm jealous if he talks with other women. I'm convinced they're more attractive, more desirable than I am.

We're in someone's loft studio, it's too crowded. I feel like I'm suffocating. Everyone is talking to everyone else, huge paintings hang on the walls, the paint laid on layer after layer—thick dark colors, blues and blacks. I can't find him. No one is talking to me. Someone gave me some mushrooms earlier and now I'm starting to come on to them, I feel jumpy and want to find something to drink to calm me down. I bump into a woman, she stares at me in dislike, turns away. I get through the crowd and pour myself some wine, drink it quickly, and pour another one, asking people if they've seen him. No one has. I'm panicked, sure he's met another woman and left with her.

I go into the bathroom and lock the door. I feel sick so I crouch at the toilet but I can't throw up. Sitting down on the floor, my back against the wall, I stare at the postcards tacked above the toilet. I know I'm seeing images but I can't tell my brain what they are, specifically; they're like abstract paintings, they have no meaning. I feel violated by images, I can't help seeing them on billboards, on TV, in ads and movies, they get into me through osmosis and change my thought patterns: what I'm supposed to look like, feel like, be. I close my eyes and see blue snowflakes.

He's pounding on the door, his voice sounds far away. I get up and open it. He takes me in his arms.

Please fuck me, I say. Fuck me here, on the floor.

He locks the door and undresses me. I lie down on the floor; it's cold, I'm shivering. He takes off his shirt and tucks it under me. He's standing over me, unzipping his black leather pants. I start hallucinating that he's a demon, his eyes are frightening—dark brown, he's wearing his contacts so there's a yellowish ring around his irises. I realize I don't trust him, I'm afraid he'll hurt me. I want him to hurt me.

Slap me.

He slaps me across the face. I feel myself clench, get wet. My head lolls to the side; he looks in my eyes, I'm naked, I'm begging him to do it again. He takes a condom from his pants pocket and puts it on, then slaps me again and enters me. I start to come almost immediately.

Not yet, he says, and stops moving inside me.

Please, I say, thrusting up at him; I'll go crazy if I don't finish coming. He stays still while I writhe underneath him; the orgasm goes on and on, I can't seem to stop. After a while he starts fucking me again, faster and faster, he comes with a loud moan and falls all the way on top of me.

I feel secure again feeling his weight, listening to his heart slowing down.

I talk to my friend Simone on the phone; we haven't spoken for weeks. She tells me about her lover, whom she's just broken up with.

At first it was great, she says. We did things sexually we'd never done with anyone else. But then he confessed that he likes to cross-dress. I mean, I just couldn't handle it. He wanted me to pretend he had a cunt; it was too weird.

I don't talk about my sex life to Simone; at least, not the really intimate details. My girlfriends and I discuss the size of our lovers' cocks, tell each other if they're any good in bed; I told Simone about the time I met two guys in North Beach and went to the Holiday Inn with them. Simone likes being tied up, but I don't want to talk about it with her. He and I have our own private world, we spend hours together absorbed in each other, seeing how far we can go. We close the curtains, nothing gets in. I tell Simone I want to marry him.

You're kidding, Simone says. How long have you known this guy?

Ten weeks.

Forget it, Simone says.

No, I mean it. I've been with enough men. I don't want to do that anymore.

The Virtuous Woman, Simone says.

Something like that.

You can't do it. You know how you are—if you like some-body and he wants you, you let him fuck you.

But I never felt like this about anybody else. And he's the best lover I ever had, I know I couldn't find anybody else who does what he does for me.

It's not about better, Simone says. Sooner or later you'll want something different, something he can't give you, and you'll go out looking for it. And anyway, you're confusing sex with love. You're hot for this man so you think you love him.

I wonder why Simone does this to me; she can't be happy for me, she always finds flaws. She says she's just being my friend, trying to protect me. I don't call Simone for weeks because I'm afraid she'll convince me that she's right.

The more I fuck him, the more I want him; I've never had this much sex with anyone before. It's all we do—sex, work, eat, sleep. Sometimes we don't get around to cooking dinner until midnight, and sometimes we end up at two A.M. eating cheese and olives and pita bread in bed. Simone tells my other friends I'm obsessed. He's late for work all the time, his boss blames it on me. No one understands us. There's a conspiracy against us, to separate us. Romantic love is always tragic; the lovers can't stay together, death or lies or fate separates them. It's dangerous to be erotic, then you aren't so trapped; if you do it in public they look at you and their minds are filthy so they see filth, then they try to put you in jail.

After a few more weeks we quit our jobs and move to a hotel in the Tenderloin where we can be together all the time; between us we have enough money for about four months. I don't know what's going to happen after that and I don't care. I set up my tubes of paints, my chalks and charcoals and brushes, on a table in the corner of the room, and he models for me. We have a small refrigerator with a freezer that keeps tiny ice cubes frozen in plastic trays, a hot plate, an indoor barbecue, a stack of books we've bought over the years meaning to read but that we never got around to; we have a portable cassette player, tapes, potted violets, and an aloe plant. We never go farther than the corner grocery half a block away. We cook or eat takeout Vietnamese food from next door. Whatever we need from the outside world, the son of the woman two doors down picks up for us. We fight sometimes. We fall more deeply in love. Underneath everything we're blissfully happy. We know how to live. All we want is for you to go away and leave us the fuck alone.

# Fuck Yer Dinner

*Diana Eve Caplan*

It had been a whole goddamn week and still, there it was again. Shelly slapped a big pinkish orange thing on my plate with a pile of canned beans next to it. Veggie dogs for dinner. I mean, what's a goddamn veggie hot dog anyhow? Those are kinda mutually exclusive words, you know?

It was bad enough that Shelly wasn't around much no more, always out spending nights with her new friends. Always out bowling with some gal named Rhonda. Shelly and me hadn't had sex in...what was it? Two years? Three years? Who could remember after five years of marriage? After five years, ain't nothing new. I don't care what no book, no video, no new-age therapists say—after five years of marriage, it's all downhill. Ain't no hope of rekindling sparks, no matter what kind of fools you make of yourselfs buying stupid guides and giving stupid "love coupons." After five years of marriage, changes in your wife don't seem like new territories being discovered. Just seem like hassles. Like...goddamned veggie dogs.

I'd eaten meat every damn night of my natural life. Roast beef, roast turkey, roast chicken, meat loaf, steak. Ribs at the corner smokehouse. And real hot dogs. Ballpark ones—plump when you cook 'em, bursting fulla cow and pig juice.

"I ain't eating this crap no more, Shelly. I want some real dinner. And I want it now." I ain't never bossed Shelly around none, but I figured it was a good time to start. This vegetarian stuff was killin' me. Specially since Shelly hadn't gotten round yet to figuring out how to cook nothing vegetarian but those damned veggie dogs. Don't know what made her go all hippie on me, anyway.

I thumped my fist on the table. "I mean it, Shelly. I ain't messing around. I want some meat. I want dinner my way. Now!" I stood there waiting, kinda scared of what Shelly was gonna do.

"You want dinner, Lou? What's the matter with what I made, huh? Not like you ever taste anything I cook for you anyway, the way you gulp it down like an animal. It's usually about how *much* food you got, Lou, not what it *tastes* like. So how's about I boil up another four or five of these smart pups for your dinner, you big hog? How's that?"

She'd never been so mouthy before. Must be that damn Rhonda, telling her to back talk. Goddamn feminazis. I hate when gals get together. Just making a buncha trouble for honest hardworking guys, you know? So I thumped my fist on the table, and did something I never done before—picked up her crystal vase of daisies or roses or some shit like that, and I heaved it against the wall. Shattered all over the floor. Got a rush in me when I did it—felt good saying how I felt, you know? And I yelled, "Fuck yer dinner, Shelly! Just fuck it!" Well, heck, Shelly stared at me and my heart just about stopped. There was a look on her face I'd never seen before. I almost thought she was gonna grab a knife and lunge at me. But she didn't. Instead, she walked into the next room, into our bedroom. I heard her opening and slamming drawers and tossing stuff around. Thought maybe she was having a fit with my clothes so they wouldn't look ironed none no more. And I started to get even more pissed, 'cuz it's real important to me that when I walk onto the showroom floor, me and my suits look as snazzy as the used cars. Makes customers feel more confident when we look crisp and clean.

"What the hell you doin' in there, Shelly? Get outta there now—you just about done enough pissing me off for one night and I'm 'bout ready to throw yer butt out onto the street. That'll teach ya to behave."

And then Shelly came out, toting some goddam contraption on an extension cord. Looked like a skinny white ET with this ribbed bulbous thing at the top and a little flare at the bottom with this long cord sticking out. Looked kinda like that thumper vibrating thing my old crackpot chiropractor used on me when I threw my back out that one time, bending down to pick up some old gum wrappers and stuff from the floor of the driver side before a customer got in to take a spin.

"Fuck yer dinner, huh, Lou? Fuck yer dinner? Fine, I'll show you fuck yer dinner."

Maybe at another time in my life, maybe when I was younger, I woudda known how to handle the situation, but I didn't. I thought for sure that Shelly had lost all her nuts and bolts and all I could do was watch. She jammed the plug into an outlet, ripped down her pants, and rubbed that thing all buzzing and shaking against her bare...womanhood. Only took near about five seconds, and her hips started rocking more than they ever did after a long, steady five minutes of me pumping in her, the way I did just before I was about to...you know. Just watching her hips rock like that, I felt like the crazy old bat was trying to seduce me or something and I felt myself grow...well, I got a woody, despite how crazy it was, what she was doing. Then she grabbed that veggie dog—it was one of them bigger veggie dogs tonight since I'd complained fake dogs were so much smaller than real hot dogs—and she jammed that veggie dog right up inside herself. Swear to God and the Blessed Virgin, she did. Didn't have to spit on it first or anything; it slid right in. She dropped to her knees on the floor, not even looking at me, and she jammed that fake wiener in and out, in and out, moaning real loud, louder than she ever done with me. Imagine that, a hot dog, and a fake one at that. I was embarrassed, thinking maybe the neighbors might hear or come peek through the window to see what was happening. Maybe they thought I was killing her or something.

"I'm fucking yer dinner, just like you asked!" she yelled, rubbing that machine against her so fast and hard that her...womanhood...lips looked human, like human lips singing, but big ones, all swollen and red like they were covered in bright lipstick and I wanted more than ever before to go to her, to pump like crazy, to pump because watching her was like watching somebody standing ready to throw a baseball without anyone to bat it or catch it, and that's just wrong. Shelly needed a man. Shelly needed me.

But suddenly I couldn't move because somehow it dawned on me that maybe she wasn't thinking about me. Maybe not. She was screwing herself with my dinner and maybe she liked it, maybe she didn't care none that I was standing right there. Her body wracked and shuddered; I'm sure she came, and I thought, Thank God at least it's over now. I thought maybe we'd just pretend like it never happened, but then her body wracked hard again and she kept bucking against that thing. She ripped off her shirt and squeezed her tits 'til they turned purple, and even shoved a finger up her own rear and all I could do was stand and watch like an idiot. It was like she could just come and come and keep coming, and then finally she whipped that veggie dog out and started sucking the damn thing, sucking it and snorting like she wanted to drink off her own, you know, and I just...I just didn't know what in the heck to do about that. For a minute I thought, well shit, maybe I ought to loosen up a bit and try some of those damn love coupons with her. You know—do things that were new and exciting. But where would I draw the line? Would I be able to? Would I want to? I started to move toward her, just started to move a smidgen when she growled and grunted, "Stay back, Lou. I don't need your help. I been learning all kinds of new tricks with Rhonda and the girls. Don't you touch me, you big animal, or you'll ruin a perfectly good orgasm."

Shit, and I thought she'd done come already.

# The Education of Professor Puppy
*Raphaela Crown*

"Of *course* she's a dyke," Josh was insisting, as we lay in my new brass bed reading the Sunday *Des Moines Register* and lazily exploring each other. I had looped the tie of my bathrobe suggestively over one bedpost, but Josh had failed to take the hint.

"Lesbian," I corrected automatically. "I think only lesbians are allowed to call each other dykes. Anyway, don't be ridiculous—she's married. And Helen and François have a terrific relationship—aren't they always talking about how great it is that François had a vasectomy?"

"For a woman who has a doctorate in English, you can be pretty naive sometimes, Puppy," Josh replied, ruffling my hair. "The woman is hot for you. God, they call this a paper? How can you be living in Iowa?"

"Technically, I don't have my doctorate yet," I pointed out, "not till after my defense. And besides, you think everyone is hot for me." It was true, he did—it was one of his best features. But I hated having my hair ruffled, even if I already had bed hair. And I hated being reminded of how naive I was.

At twenty-six, two months into my first real teaching job, I knew I was not a very credible professor—even of the assistant variety, even at obscure-but-respectable Valmont College. To make matters worse, I was still carrying around my ridiculous childhood nickname—Puppy—bestowed, as family legend had it, when my three-year-old brother looked into my crib and howled in disappointment, "I wanted a puppy!" Of course my mother delighted in calling me Professor Puppy.

"You *are* hot, Pups," Josh murmured. Satisfied that he'd made his point, he flicked the paper aside and dove under the quilt. I was usually a big fan of Josh's efforts at cunnilingus— the man truly loved to lick—but now his beard felt scratchy and rough against my thighs. All at once a picture of Helen's white, smooth skin floated into my mind. I took back the tie and put on my bathrobe.

"Let's go test drive the new Rabbit," I suggested. "Yes, of course you can drive."

Our inability to get the Sunday *New York Times* on Sunday notwithstanding, I had tried to persuade Josh that Valmont, Iowa, was an oasis of sophistication and urbanity. Helen and François were Exhibit A.

But Josh was not nearly as taken as I was with my new friends, whom he insisted on calling Inspector Clouseau and Madame Frigidaire. I explained that well-bred WASPs often seemed chilly—it was just their way. Helen *was* remarkably...cool. She looked like Amelia Earhart, with the same classily boyish features. She even wore aviator glasses and white silk scarves, though of course many of us were wearing them in 1988. On Helen, though, they seemed less like fashion and more like a calling. She often seemed to be gazing out in the distance—perhaps checking weather conditions—so that when her glance finally settled on you, it felt like a gift from the heavens. François, on the other hand, was a Frenchman out of Central Casting: buggy eyes, small moustache, even a beret, which he wore without irony. Helen laughed that when he went off to teach in the morning she always expected to see a baguette under his arm in place of his briefcase.

"He's hot for you, too, you know," Josh added, as cornstalk after cornstalk sped by.

"Please, Josh, this is ridiculous," I answered, trying to distract him by putting my hand on his zipper. But all he said was, "Great idea, Pup, but not while I'm driving—ooh, nice downshift."

Josh was finishing up his residency at Columbia, where we'd shared a cramped studio apartment until I'd moved to Iowa. We were a modern liberated couple, taking turns commuting. Though I was often apprehensive about his coming to visit—Valmont seemed silly, not quaint, when I saw it through his eyes—I was always sad to see him leave. The problem was that Josh was just too suitable: smart, handsome, decent, with a bright, affluent future ahead of him. My friends called him the Jewish mother's dream, but I loved him anyway. I just wasn't ready to be the wife of a successful specialist, to spend my days awash in the anxieties of the prosperous: What model Volvo? Which private school? Nanny or *au pair?* Besides, I would soon have a doctorate in English from Columbia and could deconstruct with the best of them.

But the truth is that, for all my declarations of independence, I was lonely and terrified. I had landed in a foreign land. And the natives thought that *I* was the alien. All I had to do was ask the dry cleaners, "When will these be ready?" and the proprietor would reply, "You're not from around here, are you?"

Fortunately, Helen and François took me under their wing. Helen was in my department, a specialist in eighteenth century lit; François, of course, taught French. I often found myself in their charming but decaying Victorian house, enjoying their bilingual children—not far from my age—and François's excellent cooking.

The usual postdinner activity involved retiring to a den hidden in the basement while the kids went out with their friends. There would be more wine, some dope, and soon we would be leaning against the couches rather than actually sitting on them.

On one such night the three of us stumbled out of the basement to see *Dangerous Liaisons* at the Valmont Bijoux. I was mesmerized by the film, which may explain why at first I failed to notice François's hand creeping up my thigh. As he advanced on one flank—literally—Helen began on the other. His pressure increased, then hers. I shifted, shocked and turned on; François crept inward. Soon Helen had traveled up my wrist, then transferred my arm to her lap. As she brushed the tips of my fingers with hers, François moved in. Two snake fingers entered my panties from below, siphoned off the juice, then went back, lubricated, for my clit. While my left arm swatted him away, my hips lifted to give him fuller access. Meanwhile, back on the right, Helen was sucking my index finger, then trailing my hand over her very prominent nipples.

Somewhere, in another country, people were watching the movie. Surely they noticed my heavy breathing, the strong smell emanating from my seat? Suddenly the lights went on—the movie had ended without my realizing. I was ushered into Helen and François's Citroen. Wordlessly, we drove to my house, François's erection bumping against my ass as he followed me up the stairs. The two of them sat down rather primly on the couch while I went into the kitchen to find us something to drink.

I remembered, vaguely, that glasses were generally kept in cupboards and that there was probably white wine in the refrigerator. I was bent over in front of the fridge when François came in, lifted my skirt, then leaned me up against the counter.

"Now I fuck you," he said, pushing down my underwear and opening his pants. With one hand he lifted me onto his prick; with the other he opened my blouse and dug for my tits, pinching and squeezing them, as he thrust into me from behind. I was stunned by the size of him. His fat balls slapped against my ass, their heaviness pushing me toward orgasm. I came even before he did, and didn't notice that Helen had entered the kitchen. I leaned against the counter, panting and dripping—then turned around to see her kneeling, licking François's wet cock as delicately as a cat. The huge prick turned out to be uncircumcised—the first I'd ever seen.

I had been faintly attracted to women from time to time. But I had never before been so assaulted by desire for anyone. Helen's taut ass, her straight back, the extraordinary contrast between her composed, dignified features and her rapt attention to her husband's penis, all were far more arousing than anything I'd ever seen or imagined.

I didn't know what the rules were for this sort of thing—if there were rules for this sort of thing. I knew only that I had to touch her, had to taste her mouth, her cunt. I don't remember how we ended up in bed, my blouse open but my skirt still on, Helen naked and straddling my mouth. But I remember the moment I moved from her outer lips to the peat moss inside—the taste as deep and dark as unfiltered scotch.

I wanted to be in her and around her at the same time, to lick and tease and plunge all at once. I loved how she shimmied as my flat tongue slowly slid along her cunt, how she shuddered when my thumb went up inside her, my fingers circling her clit. I wanted to pull her body onto mine, to suffocate in her wet folds.

François wanted to fuck. He immediately saw the possibilities of the bedposts and tied my wrists to them with Helen's long silk scarf. Then he lay his wife on top of me and entered her from behind. As he pushed into her, she pushed into me; soon we were all heaving together.

In bed afterward, it was strangely familiar, like seeking refuge with my parents during a thunderstorm. But it was also faintly creepy. These people were old enough to be my par-ents—*were* parents. They were not comforting me during a thunderstorm but bringing me to orgasm after orgasm.

Night after night, they made me come again—and again. François loved to rub "his women" together like sticks, watch us ignite, then fuck one or both of us from behind. Eventually he would fall asleep, while Helen and I feasted on each other.

When I next went to see Josh in New York, I tried to ration my references, taking care not to mention Helen or François too much—or suspiciously too little. But while the world had once seemed oppressively organized into couples, it now seethed with secret trios. I spent hours in the video store searching for the right romantic comedy for us to watch and came back holding *Sunday Bloody Sunday*.

On my return, François and Helen assumed that we would simply resume.

"How was the Jewish doctor?" François asked with an unattractive grin. "Did you take him in your mouth, Puppy, did you suck him till he came?" I saw the glint in his eyes before I noticed his erection. I fingered the note Helen had left in my mailbox: *I haven't told him I'm in love with you. I am, you know*.

"I don't want to play anymore," I heard myself announce, trying to catch Helen's eye.

"But one last time, surely," he suggested.

I realized I didn't like him very much, but was willing to have sex with him, knowing he would soon go to sleep and I could be with Helen.

That night her lovemaking seemed wistful, yet more ardent than before. Over and over she bent her head to my breast, nuzzling and suckling. Once again I shivered as her ice melted, thrilled at the power I had to make her thaw. "I can't be with-out you," I whispered. "Ah, Puppy," she said, "I'd hoped...."

I was driving my new car. We plunged into the Iowa countryside, Helen fingering me as I bucked and groaned at sixty miles an hour. The cornstalks had all been cut down.

I was drunk on sex. I lived only to make Helen come. I loved the look on her face when she threw her head back and actually laughed with amazement at her own pleasure. In one ghastly restaurant after another—all featuring fried pork loin—I would take my stockinged foot and explore her crotch under the table, while she told me sternly what a bad girl I was. Then she would tell me what she would do when she was free to enter me. As I squirmed in my seat, she would lick her fingers and slowly rim the glass.

"Does your beautiful boy do this, Puppy?" she would ask. "Or this?" Then we would run for the nearest bathroom, movie theater, car, desperate to finish what we could not seem to stop. We would declare the impossibility of our liaison and vow to break it off—then find ourselves in the Thrifty Scot Motel for two hours of expensive pleasure. Helen would appear at my office, always with book in hand to "return," in case someone was with me; we would kiss leaning up against the door to prevent it from being opened accidentally, but then rattle it loudly with our thrusts.

I was increasingly evasive with Josh and failed to come to New York as scheduled. I pleaded a cold—the short commuter flight to Chicago would hurt my ears. No, there was no point in his coming here; "too much work," I said.

"Then I'll come there," he said. "Is it her? Is it him? Just tell me, for God's sake, Puppy!"

"Don't be silly," I replied. "He's a horrible man. Anyway, don't worry, we'll see each other soon."

I tried to pry myself from between Helen's legs long enough to appraise my situation realistically. I loved Josh. Inwardly I reviewed the litany of his virtues: He was smart, decent, handsome, devoted; he would do anything to make me happy. Was I going to throw all that away—*him*—for sexual high jinks with some dissolute academic? It didn't make sense. And yet the siren call of Helen's thighs—the surge of sexual power when I held her down, the gutwrenching, terrifying joy of letting her tie me up, of putting my trust in this untrustworthy but literally captivating lover—how could I give *that* up? How could I go back to Josh's spirited but conventional lovemaking, the one man–one woman prison of eternal monogamy?

On the other hand, the situation with Helen was fraught with peril. Besides, the Ice Woman was showing definite signs of cracking. She was increasingly paranoid—François suspected, she thought. The next day she was sure he knew. We would have to stop. Perhaps one last kiss. There was one last kiss, then another—soon I was on the kitchen floor while Helen drilled her perfectly manicured fingers into me. Oddly, as I came, I thought of Josh's sturdy prick.

The day I was supposed to go to New York but didn't, Helen appeared at my house in tears. François had followed her to my house, a terrible scene had ensued. She had betrayed him, broken the rules, mistaken sex play for real life. And she was sorry to tell me this, but François had called Josh in revenge and told him all about his wayward girlfriend.

I started to cry—with relief, sorrow, loss. Josh finally knew. Now I would have to decide—maybe there was nothing left to decide. Helen slowly unbuttoned my blouse, snaked off my tight skirt, then unwound her scarf, tying my hands to the bedposts. Still clothed, she began to lick me, moving slowly up one thigh, circling lightly around my clit, then traveling down again. "Let me touch you, please," I begged, as her elegant tongue continued its relentless teasing. I lifted my hips up, desperate to push against something hard and unyielding, but she continued to lick and nibble till I was bucking the air. Finally she plunged her long fingers in and fucked me, hard; I came against her hand, and again as she withdrew her wet fingers and replaced them with her lips. Then she pulled off her silky trousers and lowered herself onto my face, her own hands cupping her white breasts.

Perhaps that's why I didn't hear Josh come in. Or maybe I did hear him. Maybe I wanted him to hear Helen's shout as she ground herself against my mouth, then fell back against my belly. Maybe I wanted him to see me covered in my lover's juices. Maybe I wanted him to see me as I was—ashamed and excited, my body and desires fully exposed.

Josh stood there looking at me, his expression unreadable. "So, is this what you want—women? bondage?" he demanded.

I turned my head away, then looked straight at him. "It's not all I want," I answered, "but yes."

"Well, why didn't you say something, Pup?" he replied, loosening his tie.

I watched, stunned, as Josh calmly removed his clothes, then lowered himself onto Helen. I didn't have to ask what *he* wanted; his erection was huge. Helen put her arms around his neck, then wrapped her long legs around him. I watched Josh's tight ass move up and down, faster and faster, Helen clinging to him for dear life. Though my part of the bed was heaving along with them, they seemed to take no notice of me. Wait a second, I thought. Aren't *I* supposed to be the pivot here?

"Yes, yes, *yes!*" she was soon shouting, as she covered his neck with eager, frenetic kisses. Great, I thought—now she's Molly Bloom. Josh's orgasmal shout was less literary—he grunted, loud, then fell back on top of her.

I couldn't stand it. This was *my* boyfriend, fucking *my* lover. I pulled my wrists free, then burrowed between them, frantically seeking out Josh's wet, soft prick with my mouth.

"Hi, Pup," he said softly, just a hint of triumph in his voice.

"Well, you weren't *totally* right about Helen," I mumbled, as he grew between my lips.

"Didn't your mother ever tell you not to talk with your mouth full? Oh, Pup, you are *so* hot," he murmured, his prick already hard.

"But I've been very bad," I answered.

"I know," he said. "Tell me all about it," he added, reaching for his tie.

# A Letter I Will Never Send

### Katherine Love

Claire, I just realized that in the four months we've lived on the same floor of this apartment building, you haven't worn a skirt until today. You've started shaving your legs! My, how things have changed since college. Funny that you were the one who hated my identification as "bisexual" while we were dating, and now you have a husband and I haven't touched a man in six years aside from my clients. Funny how things work out.

You look good in that skirt, Claire. Subtle, professional, and you've still got great legs. I hope you don't mind that I was staring at you in the elevator. I can't believe you get away with that long hair. Your one vanity, eh? From lesbian separatist to poster girl for Miss Business America, and you still have the blond springs of Goldilocks. Only you could pull it off, Claire, only you. Even at five foot three, with pale skin and eyes of innocent blue diamonds, there is something so no-nonsense about you. Maybe it's your curt voice and your sharp walk. You always have every paper and index card in order, every fairy-tale curl in place. You enter a room with a suit and a briefcase, and I would be terrified to defy you. And when you're wearing nothing but black satin lingerie....

I wonder how far up you shave. I wonder if you shave everything. I wonder if you even wax those dark black hairs that circle your nipples. God, I hope you don't.

I wish I could ask you. Two years ago I suppose I would have just done it. I would've watched you squirm uncomfortably as your voice rejected my question with polite reserve, and I would have enjoyed it. Enjoyed it until it started to hurt, and then I would've told you in desperate whispers how often I still fantasize about you. How much I have missed you. How no one I've been with has taken your place.

And you, Claire? What do you think about me? When you first saw me, stepping out of the elevator with arms full of boxes, there was a pause before you laughed and said, "small world," and offered me a cup of tea. But I saw your face in that pause. I saw your shock. I saw you remember.

And when I told you I'd cleaned up and gone back to school, you said, "I always knew you would." You said it so softly, so tenderly, that for a moment I almost forgot you were lying.

Your husband's a nice guy, Claire. It was sweet of him to invite me over for dinner when all my kitchen utensils were still scattered in boxes and I was living off pizza and Chinese take-out. He's a pleasant guy. Boring, but pleasant. And he's not a bad cook either. I do hope you're happy with him; I really do.

I had a good chuckle when he asked if I was an athlete. I honestly don't think he caught on to how you were staring at my body, do you, Claire? Does he know you're attracted to women? I noticed that you told him we were good friends from college, and never mentioned that we used to share a bed, or that we had planned to spend our lives together.

And you told him I wasn't an athlete, but a writer, never mind how I make my money. You know, I've only published one story, and I don't think I ever mentioned it to you. You must have found it on your own. How did it strike you to suddenly see my name, especially in that kind of anthology?

Your husband didn't even ask what kinds of things I wrote, so I asked you, while he was absorbed with chewing his food, what you thought of my story. And you caught my eye and winked when you answered, "It was very...effective."

Oh, Claire, when you said that I was surprised I didn't leave a puddle on your smooth wooden seat. I know how you read erotica. I can picture you vividly. You lie in the bathtub with my story clutched in one hand, and then it slips from your fingers onto the bath mat as your knees climb the wall's white tiles and your ass slides toward the running faucet. Your hair is unleashed and frizzing wildly in the steam, flying out as if you're posed in front of a fan. You don't make noise when you masturbate, but your chin lifts slightly, and your eyelashes flutter shut. As your body pulses to climax, your face takes on this expression of intense concentration, as if you expect to be asked about the experience on the bar exam, and you want to catch every detail.

God, Claire, I know you so well. I know I can't have you back, can't manufacture some crisis and run to you sobbing the way I used to do in college, believing I couldn't control myself, whispering, "Just hold me, please, I need you," until you were crying too and promising you would love me forever. I know better now; life isn't a movie. Still, sometimes I can't believe he makes you as happy as I could. I know things about you he could never understand. He doesn't remember the time you convinced twenty students to boycott Mr. Simon's political philosophy class because he called on women less than men. He didn't feel you trembling the first time your fingers felt the inside of another woman's body. Do you remember, Claire? And how, in the morning, you woke up and smiled at me and said, "Morning, beautiful," and I smiled back and said, "Hi, ugly," and you laughed until you rolled off the bed? I bet he doesn't make you laugh like that. I bet he never lets you paint pictures on his back with menstrual blood. I bet he doesn't make love to you on public elevators between floors while leaning on the button that keeps the doors closed.

You remember *that*, Claire, I know you do. The morning I went out for breakfast, and you were on your way to work, and we took the elevator at the same time, I looked at you as I pressed that button, and you blushed. The whole ride down we didn't talk or look at each other, but you had goose bumps, and I could hear your breath. We stood close without touching, but you wanted to, as much as I did; I could feel it. I've never been closer to going down on my knees and taking your hand and begging you, *Run away with me. Things will be like they were.* But I didn't, because they wouldn't be. Everything is different. You have framed paintings and photographs on your walls, and I've still got the same fucking posters from college, held up with scotch tape. In some ways, I don't know anything about you. We never talk unless I see you in the laundry room or the elevator. You have a career, a husband, a reputation. Your friends don't go to sex parties. And Jesus, my friends would probably hate you.

Besides, I'm used to living alone. I'm used to having my own space and following my own schedule, freely bringing women to my bed at any time of day or night. I've learned a lot since college. I bet you've never been fisted, Claire.

I've noticed that you avoid being alone with me in my apartment. I've had dinner with you and your husband twice, but if I invite you in for coffee, you always find some excuse. Are you afraid of me?

Why, Claire? Are you afraid you'll turn around and suddenly feel your back pressed to the wall, my hips flush against yours; afraid you'll feel my fingers clenching your princess hair and my breath hissing "Submit" into your ear?

I can't say I haven't thought about it.

It would be so different now, Claire. We wouldn't giggle self-consciously for twenty minutes, trying to get the strap-on at the right angle. I would know how to handle you. I understand your need to be seized and then worshiped. You always wanted to be the romance-novel heroine, even when you dressed like an androgynous dyke. I'd kiss you and you'd fall limp in surrender.

God, what it was like to kiss you.

This time there would be no giddy laughter. There would be only sharp breaths as I squeezed your nipple and my other hand grasped your thigh. I'd tease your flesh until you were dripping through your pantyhose, and then I'd tear the nylon clean off your body.

I'd be weak and ready to fall at your feet, but I wouldn't let you know it. I'd make sure you were the one on your knees. Oh yes, Claire. I'd want to see your pretty lips around my cock as I tugged again on a fistful of your sunny curls.

And then I'd lay you down gently on the bed and remove the rest of your clothing. You would lie still and dazed, your blue eyes wide, not sure what to expect from me. I'd trade rough kisses for soft ones. I'd put my arms around you and press my lips to your stomach. I'd kiss zigzags across your neck and breasts and punctuate them with soft bites. And I'd hear you sigh and murmur and just as your body began to relax under me, I'd spread your legs. I would penetrate you, suddenly, harshly, and you'd grab my shoulder and dig fingernails into my back. And I'd fuck you, Claire, all night if necessary. I'd fuck you until you felt all of your fingers and toes tingling. I'd fuck you until all of your curls were disheveled, and that look of concentration would be broken, and your throat would fill with wails.

If only, Claire. The things I would do if we were younger, and had nothing to lose.

# Shadow Child
## Cheyenne Blue

She has always followed people, slipping through the shadows in their wake, pattering on soft-shod feet in and out of darkness and pools of light, daring them to turn and see her.

When she was small, she would follow her mother around the house, peering out of closet doors and spying under the shower curtain at her mother's dimpled and voluptuous figure shaving her legs in the shower.

"Adrienne?" Her mother's tired voice, separating each syllable of her name, rising up at the end in warning, would result in cascading giggles through chubby fingers and inevitably the wide-eyed horror of the chase, the capture, and the punishment.

But even the humiliation of a red, stinging bottom would not stop her stalking. She would watch her mother, plump thighs spread on the toilet bowl, belly quivering, the wipe of the brown furred gash with the pink paper. She would watch her brother, fingering his pee-pee, playing with the pinched tip and the hairless empty sacs of skin that hung below.

Daringly, she followed her third-grade teacher out of school, into the parking lot. She slunk into the back seat of her car when the teacher placed books and papers on the passenger seat and fumbled for the dropped keys at her feet. Huddled on the floor, feeling the thrum of the drive shaft under her cheek on the puppy-pee–smelling carpet, Adrienne rode home with her teacher, creeping out of the unlocked car in the darkened garage long after dinnertime.

As a teenager the thrill of the hunt fully enraptured her. Brett the bastard, Brett the unfaithful, Brett the pubescent hero who captured her imagination and taught her what the space between her legs was really for. Hurried encounters on the cracked vinyl seats of his Chevy, the faded floral upholstery of his parents' couch, and once, daringly, in their bed.

"Hurry," she would whisper in mock terror in his ear as he heaved and grunted above her. "We'll get caught."

Brett the bastard, who used the constant fear of discovery as an excuse to evade her satisfaction. "It takes too long, Addy," he would say, shaking his head in pretend sympathy when she guided his hand to her aching center. "They'll catch us."

Brett the unfaithful, who had time aplenty to pleasure her best friend, with his hands and with his mouth. Those same twisted thin lips that he would never place on her, Addy, not where she wanted it most.

She suspected him of infidelity, and in the hot haze of teenage jealousy followed him one night, in black jeans and black sweatshirt, her bright hair caught under a dark cap: the spy, the wronged one, sick and heartsore.

She remembers well how the thump of her heart drowned out her soft footfalls on rain-soaked streets. She followed him, flitting in and out of doorways, a vampire child in black merging with the shadows, dodging the shimmering pools of street lights. It was too easy. Brett the arrogant never looked back, just walked with purposeful stride to his assignation. The dark dead-end alley, that cliché of spy stories, the garbage bins, the metal fire escape, even, she saw, the flick of a rat's tail.

She waited, hidden in the shadow of a fire escape, and watched in clenching horror as her friend approached. Brett the betrayer grabbed her friend around the waist, his mouth descending to claim, his hands moving to her breasts.

It was fast and it was urgent. It was heated. It was everything she'd never had. She watched as his mouth moved on soft, white breasts, biting and sucking with fevered urgency, his hands popping buttons, curling down into lace panties. She watched her friend rip open his fly, free his cock, wrap her small hand around the shaft, and stroke it rhythmically. She saw the thrust of that cock repeatedly into the hand, the clench of the buttocks, the guttural cries of completion, and the spill of the seed over the hand, over the cloth, and onto the ground. Brett the selfish dropped to his knees, flaccid cock drooping out of his pants, and put his mouth to her friend. She saw the blonde head roll back in ecstasy as he slurped and suckled her, howls of release echoing in the empty alley.

Adrienne's hand was down her own pants, snaking into her sodden panties, parting her curls with a delicate finger to probe up, into the heat and moisture of her arousal. She watched, panting, as Brett the philanderer drove his renewed hardness into her friend, thrusting and grinding, pressing her back against the wet stone of the alleyway, pumping into her with the short, hard spurts she knew so well.

She came when he did, her flickering finger and the sight of his urgent thrusts driving her over the edge into the silent spasms of release.

They passed her as they left, hand in hand. She turned her face from them so that its pale oval wouldn't give her presence away. She didn't want them to find her here, jeans undone, panties twisted and soaked with her juices.

She followed them at other times too. Compulsively into their secret hideaways in bleachers and alleys, in drive-ins and park bushes. It was too easy. And it was better than Brett the uncaring ever was.

She has always followed people, slipping through the shadows in their wake, pattering on soft-shod feet in and out of darkness and pools of light, daring them to turn and see her.

Now she follows strangers. It is an altogether different proposition, fraught with risk and the dangers of discovery. She has a sixth sense that tells her when someone is just sliding off to be alone and when they are off to meet a lover or husband. She cannot define it; maybe it's the release of musk and pheromones into the air, maybe it's that yeasty smell of arousal; maybe she has become so attuned to the gestures of secrecy that she knows them without conscious thought. Whatever it is, she is rarely wrong.

Adrienne waits outside the glass monolith. An office building like many others, nondescript in its conformity of sleek and soulless design. Her latest vicarious lover works here, and he will be leaving soon, leaving to meet his lover. She wonders what he tells his wife, what apologetic story of work and deadlines he will weave to cover his deception.

She watches him leave, striding into the windblown street, head lowered, dark trousers flapping around his legs. The colors of fall surround him: russet leaves, pumpkin-orange candy wrappers—and Adrienne's fox-red head as she slip-streams in his wake.

He enters a church. It is unlocked at this hour, although later it will be barred against the homeless who sleep under its lintels. She slips in behind him, creeping into a pew in the middle, falling to her knees on the hassock and peering through laced fingers at her prey as he hesitates, looking around before he slips into the vestibule at one side of the altar.

Apart from herself, Adrienne the irreverent, the church is now empty. She waits, head bowed in mock penitence until she hears the swift tapping of purposeful heels hurrying down the aisle. It's Wednesday. It's five o'clock, time for an illicit quickie. Hail Mary, mother of grace.

The heels fade into silence, entering the vestibule. Adrienne imagines the soft kiss of greeting, the rustle of hands moving over crisp business linens, the sigh against the exposed neck. She waits, counting her heartbeats. Too soon and she risks discovery. Too late and she misses the heated foreplay, the bites and the panting.

On silent feet she approaches the wooden door. Her gut clenches as she slowly pushes the door open. She offers a prayer of gratitude to whoever has kept the door so silent on its oiled hinges. A dart, a duck, a flurry of skirts, and she's in, holed up like a ferret, tucked behind the stacked music stands and trestle tables. One hand burrows under her skirt and into her panties in hot anticipation of what is to come.

She spreads her legs, and dips between them. Through the stalks of table legs and dusty surfaces she can see them. His mouth is already moving on bared breasts, the dark business suit hanging open as the infidel gropes with pale hands. A pinch of the rosy nipple, puckered and erect, quivering in anticipation. The open mouth on her breast.

"No marks," whispers the woman, then stifles a scream as he bites. A rosy bloom on the soft skin. The hot, sweet smell of arousal coils lazily into the room.

Adrienne's fingers circle her own sex, around and around, slowly, touching the tender lips with careful fingers. She mustn't come too soon. She watches through drooping lids as the man lifts the dark skirt, bunching it in his large hand. Slender legs come into view. Higher, he drags the skirt higher, sliding it over quivering thighs, the rasp of linen on nylon sending sparks of static leaping into the charged air. Adrienne fancies that they could ignite in the heated tension of the room.

The skirt is around the woman's waist now as she leans back, arched over the stacked chairs. Her lover drops to his knees and pulls stockings and panties down and off in one swift movement. His mouth drops and latches onto her, sucking on her open flushed sex. Adrienne sees the golden hands spreading the creamy thighs, sees the shining moisture as he plants his face deep into the pungent crevice, slurping loudly, swallowing, and sucking.

Her own finger dips deep into the cream of her sex, and she brings it to her mouth, tasting the salt and sour. She fixes her eyes on the man, and mimics his pistoning tongue with her finger.

The woman's orgasm is sudden. Her upper body jolts, jolts again. The little death. Her mouth forms an O, rosebud pale, funeral rose pink.

The man rises, undoes his trousers, freeing his shaft, shiny and taut with tension. Adrienne can almost feel the silky smoothness of it. She can imagine the slippery moisture oozing from the slotted tip. She is circling with two fingers now, slipping easily in and out of her own sodden sex, wet to the wrist, the tops of her thighs sticky and sweat-filmed.

He positions himself and plunges in, a smooth, sliding thrust, all the way to the hilt. The woman's hands delve down the back of his trousers, grasping his undulating buttocks, dragging him deeper and closer. She wraps a slender leg possessively around the back of his thighs, rubbing catlike over the expensive suit.

Adrienne plunges in and out with matching rhythm. Her breathing seems loud and erratic in the sepulchral room, but she knows from experience that they will not hear her. Their inner worlds are building, tension deep in the pits of their bellies consumes them, the heavy breathing of the watcher in the shadows will go unnoticed in the sweet release of climax.

Adrienne comes, shuddering through her orgasm, mouth trembling open, eyes wide, struggling to control the timbre of her breathing, struggling to fill her lungs quietly enough to avoid discovery. She spirals down from her peak, still fingering the damp curls, touching her swollen lips with a gentle finger. She likes it when she comes first, so that she can watch their conclusion unhampered.

They are nearly there. She watches as the thrusts get shorter, shuddering, straddle-legged thrusts, and then the fractured moment of climax as his thrusts become short, deep spurts. His head falls onto the woman's neck and he lies there panting for a moment.

They never indulge in the tender afterplay of lovers who truly care. The man raises his head, kisses his partner once on the lips. Then he lifts himself off, his penis damp and flaccid, and tucks it away in his pants. His partner stems the gush of semen down her thighs with her fingers, catching the viscous fluid and bringing it to her mouth.

Adrienne closes her eyes momentarily, vicariously enjoying the grassy, sour taste of freshly spilled seed. She wonders if they shower before returning to their homes, or do they tell their partners they're sweaty from the gym or the office? She wonders if they will make love to their own partners this evening after their irreverent encounter. There is nothing sacred about this sex.

He kisses the woman again briefly, then dresses and strides away without a backward glance. From her hiding place, Adrienne the shadow child holds her breath as he passes, then resumes watching the woman, who gazes after her lover, momentarily wistful. Then she wipes herself with her nylons and pulls on her panties. She takes a new pair of nylons from her bag and smoothes the creases out of the once crisp executive suit. A slash of funeral rose to the kiss-crushed lips, then she leaves, striding past the stalker in the shadows.

She has always followed people, slipping through the shadows in their wake, pattering on soft-shod feet in and out of darkness and pools of light, daring them to turn and see her.

# Promises to Keep

## Kate Dominic

Jimmy promised he wouldn't leave me. He *promised*. We was going to buy a house next to where his mama used to live in Pomona and have nice stuff and a big-screen TV. He was going to have a new car every year. I could get my hair done two times a week if I wanted and buy pretty dresses anytime. And we was going to have us lots and lots of babies. They'd have food on the table every night. Not just sandwiches with only one slice of baloney, either. Real food, with meat, and McDonald's whenever they was in the mood. The girls could get all the pretty dresses they wanted from Kmart, and a toy every time we went to the store—maybe even Hot Wheels cars, just like the boys. I told Jimmy we have to keep up with the times and women's lib and all that stuff. He told me he thought women's lib was a crock, 'cause he was always going to take care of me. Then he laughed and hugged me and he said, "You can have anything you want, babe, anything at all, when I score." And he was going to score. He had this big deal coming up out of Mexico. All he had to do was meet this guy in Texas. In two days, they'd be home.

I didn't like Texas. They're bad folks down there. Mean and cruel. But Jimmy, he just laughed and told me he had to go. He was going to score big, so I should just make myself all pretty for him for when he got back. He'd be rolling in money, and he was going to be wanting my pussy something fierce, because he didn't have no other woman but me. Just me. We was going to make it *big!* He told me to take care of the baby, too. My Jimmy, he was so proud. I wasn't going to tell him about the baby until he got back, but I was puking so bad I couldn't keep it a secret. Jimmy just grinned. He hugged me even though my mouth was dirty and he said he didn't care that I was spending my mornings bent over the toilet. He called me his sweet girl and said he'd be right back.

They're mean folks down in Texas. Cruel mean. What went down wasn't Jimmy's fault. The other guy had the gun. It was the other guy who shot that fucking cop. Jimmy held his hands up high, but it didn't matter. The cops killed the other guy, and they had to take out their being pissed on somebody. So even though Jimmy didn't hurt nobody, those fucking Texas bastards are going to kill him.

In his letters, Jimmy told me not to wait for him no more. He told me it was Texas, so they was going to kill him, for sure. He wasn't ever coming home. But I wrote to him every week anyway. I told him I was fine and that we was going to have a beautiful baby son. I was pretty sure it was going to be a boy. When it came time to pay the rent and I didn't have no money, I told him I was living with my cousin Sheila and working at Taco Bell. I said that with WIC and food stamps I was getting by. It was all lies. Sheila told me I was a stupid cunt for getting pregnant with a loser like Jimmy. She told me not to call her ever again.

I couldn't work because I was so sick, so damn sick, the whole first three months. I couldn't get welfare because I wasn't far enough along and I didn't have a place to get mail.

At the homeless shelter, they let me stay a few extra days beyond my limit, because I couldn't stop puking. They pretended they didn't notice when I couldn't make it out the door by eight A.M. each day, like the rules said. I got out the door as fast as I could, as soon as I wasn't hugging the toilet. One of the counselors felt sorry for me 'cause I was crying so much. Ellie said I could use their address just for Jimmy's letters, just for that. Then I was crying because I was so happy. Those letters kept me going.

Finally, Ellie had to tell me I couldn't stay there anymore. I was walking down Holt Avenue, trying to look brave. It was dark, but I didn't have nowhere to go, so I kept walking kind of close to the 7-Eleven. I was trying so hard not to cry and hoping I'd finally stopped puking in the mornings. I almost hadn't that morning. I had Jimmy's letter inside my bra. His lawyer had just told him those fucking Texas prosecutors were going for the death penalty. So I was walking down the street, wondering where I was going to sleep and what I'd wear tomorrow because the cops had tossed the building where I'd been stashing my stuff. This guy drove by. His car was weaving all over and he was drunk. He leaned out the window and said, "Hey, baby, wanna party?" And he flashed his wallet at me.

So I went with him. That first time, it was hard. We did it in the back seat of his car in an alley behind the supermarket. I pretended he was Jimmy, but it didn't help. He wasn't Jimmy. I was so mad he wasn't that afterward, when he passed out with his head on the seat, I wiggled out from under him and I stole all his money from his wallet and I took his rings and his watch. I even took his wedding ring, because he shouldn't have been cheating on his wife like that. My Jimmy never cheated on me.

I took that man's money and I went to the Goodwill and I bought me some sexy clothes. I'd never worn trash like that around my Jimmy. He called me his sweet girl, so I dressed sweet and pretty. I didn't want to look like the cheap crack-whores out on Holt Avenue. But things was different now. I had to take care of me and the baby. I felt dirty from turning that trick, but I needed the money. So I bought me some fancy hooker clothes, and I looked real fine in them. My boobs was big on account of my being pregnant, and my stomach wasn't showing. That night, I went out, and I did it again. I did it three times, with three different guys. But this time, they wasn't drunk, so I didn't steal from them. They paid good, though. I got me a room and I took a bath and I slept on a bed with clean white sheets. And the next night I went out again.

I still got Jimmy's mail down at the shelter, though. I'd told him that was Sheila's address, and I didn't want him to think I was moving around. I even put some money by, hoping to go visit him when the baby was born, so that he could see his son. I figured it had to be a son, but I knew it wouldn't matter to Jimmy. He'd love it anyway. My Jimmy loved babies, and he was going to love ours extra-special.

I was five months along when I got beat up. I still wasn't showing much, just a little bump that I put my hands on to cuddle when I slept. Sometimes I patted it when I was awake, too, when no one was looking. I'd finally stopped puking, but I still wasn't hungry much. So I was still pretty skinny. I was working a lot.

One night, I did this guy, and afterward, he said I took his watch. I didn't. I only stole from guys who passed out afterward. But this guy, he hurt me bad. He hit my face and he said he was going to call the cops. I was so scared he'd hurt the baby. That's what finally stopped him. He went to slug me in the gut, like he'd done my face and boobs, and I begged him to please, please not hurt my baby. He looked at me like I'd sucker punched him. He tore off my skirt. He'd just lifted it to do his business, but now he tore it off, and he said, "Holy fuck!" He stuffed all the money in his wallet in my hand and he pushed me out of the car. He told me he'd swear on a stack of Bibles he'd never seen me. And when he was locking the door in back of me and I was standing next to the dumpster in the alley crying, trying to hold what was left of my skirt closed, he looked on the floor and saw his watch. It was laying there, with the band busted, where it must have caught on his belt or something. He threw that out the window at me, and then he drove off, gunning the engine as he turned the corner.

I was still crying when the cop car drove down the alley. I only had on one shoe, and it had big heels, and I was hurting so bad anyway I couldn't run much. I just stood there crying and holding my clothes together. The cop, he told me, "Don't cry, girlie," and he gave me his handkerchief. He took me to the hospital where they patched me up. Then he took me in and booked me. He was real gentle, not like Texas cops. He was just doing his job. But even with all the money the guy gave me, I still had to do jail time to pay part of the fine. By the time I got out, my rent was late, so they'd put all my stuff out on the street, and it was all gone. All my fancy clothes and my food and my blankets and the baby clothes I was starting to put by, and the money I'd had hidden in the old Altoids tins inside my regular socks.

The only thing left was my letters from Jimmy. The box was tore open, but I found most of them, scattered by the dumpster. I cried when I found my picture of him and me together at Sheila's company barbecue just before he went to Texas. But that was all I had left except the busted watch and some frumpy clothes I got from the homeless shelter when the cops let me out. I went straight there to see if I had any letters from Jimmy. There was five, and he was upset, wanting to know why I hadn't wrote him.

The cops was nice, though. They gave me a ride to the shelter. They said it was because they weren't supposed to turn me loose on the street half-naked if they were trying to rehabilitate me from turning tricks. The one cop said I was showing so much now that they didn't have to worry about that! He was mean, but not too mean. Not like a Texas cop. This guy just made fun of me, but he gave me a ride to the homeless shelter and when I started crying, he said, "Ah, shit!" He and his partner each gave me five bucks and told me to get myself some lunch, so's the baby would be healthy.

The cop was right about not turning many tricks, though. My face had mostly healed, except where my cheekbone had been cracked. But I was getting big as a house. I pawned the watch for thirty dollars, but even before that was gone, I was back on the street. The men who wanted me now was mostly dead drunk or winos. Even the partying drunks could see I was knocked up and mostly stayed away. The winos didn't have much money unless they'd just got their disability checks. They smelled and I didn't like them, but I needed the money bad, so I fucked them.

One night, my friend Triola, she was working the street with me. She sent the good drunk ones my way if she thought she saw something better coming her way. Anyway, Triola says she got something to make it easier to fuck the winos. She told me it wouldn't hurt the baby, so I went around the corner and she lit up her pipe. I inhaled it real deep, just like she told me to. Jesus, oh, Jesus! I wanted to feel that way for the rest of my life! I was floating, and suddenly, it was almost as good as when Jimmy was with me. I felt so good that I could pretend he wasn't in Texas waiting to die. When I closed my eyes and let myself fly, it was almost like he was here with me. He was putting his arms around me and petting my belly and telling me I was his pretty girl. I let myself believe it was him taking me around the corner, out of the light. He laid me down with him and curled up next to me. And he loved me. Oh, he loved me.

I spread my legs for him and when his fingers touched me, I was so wet. He laughed and said he loved how his pretty girl got so turned on her pussy leaked sweet, sticky girl-juice for him. He couldn't fit on top of me anymore, not with the baby. So I rolled over and got up on my knees, and I pulled my skirt way up. He slid into me and I almost cried, it felt so good. I arched back up at him, crying out, "Ooh, ooh, OOOH!" and rubbing my cunt while he pumped into me from behind. He growled and pulled me up hard against him, hard, when he came. He pumped in and out on his own come, his baby-making come, and I yelled, "I love you, Jimmy!" He laughed and I came so hard my cunt muscles grabbed around his cock, like I was pulling him inside me to touch the baby like he was touching me. I felt so good, so good. And the baby was so quiet and mellow, I knew he felt good, too.

I woke up in the dirt by the dumpster in back of the laundromat. My skirt was up around my waist and my legs was sticky with dried come and my knees was skinned and my cunt hurt, deep down inside. I had to pee so bad I could hardly stand it. The baby was jumping on my bladder like crazy. So I just rolled over and pissed by the dumpster. When I touched myself, I was bleeding, but just a little bit. And my whole head hurt. Not just my cheekbone. It hurt all over. My whole damn body hurt. I didn't have any panties on, so I just pulled my skirt back down and went into the laundromat to use their bathroom to wash up. I didn't have any money, and the attendant said I couldn't use the restroom, even when I said I had to pee because of the baby, which I didn't, but I wanted to wash up. This lady felt sorry for me and asked the guy could I use the restroom just to pee, real quick, if she put two extra quarters in the dryer. The guy finally said OK, but I better make it quick. So I did. I just washed up as quick as I could. Then I thanked the lady and went back to the shelter to check my mail, but there wasn't a letter.

Jimmy wasn't writing as much anymore since I'd been in jail. His last letter had said it was OK if I had another boyfriend, because they was going to kill him down in Texas anyway. His lawyer was one of those bastards who fell asleep in court after lunch. He didn't give a shit about what happened, so long as he got his bourbon with lunch. Jimmy said he was real scared, but that it helped to know me and the baby was OK. He said even if I had a new boyfriend, would I please tell the baby about him when the baby was old enough to understand that his daddy had loved him so much, even though he never met him.

I wrote back that I didn't have a boyfriend. There was nobody but him. That was pretty much true. I didn't love anybody but Jimmy. I just had to work if I was going to take care of me and the baby. I told him I was going to try to come and visit when the baby was born. He said it was OK if I didn't. But would I please just send a picture. I promised him I would, and I told him I loved him so much. And that night, I went back to the corner with Triola.

Pretty soon, I was doing the white stuff all the time. I wasn't so sure as Triola that it wouldn't hurt the baby. But I had to work, and I hated the winos, and I hurt so much inside, so much. As the stuff seared into my lungs, all of a sudden my face didn't hurt so bad. No matter who came by, I could pretend he was Jimmy. I could pull my skirt up and get up on my knees and open my cunt and the hard, hot dick slamming into me was Jimmy's. He fucked me the way he used to, over and over, until my pussy hummed and I came so hard. Even when his come was dripping out of me, he'd get hard again and then he was sliding into me and fucking me. He fucked me so hard I could feel him banging up against the baby, like he was saying hello. The baby got jumpy and then he got quiet. My Jimmy kept fucking me and it felt so good.

After the first night, Triola kind of kept an eye out for me. If I was really whacked, she took the winos' money before we went around the corner. She only kept some—her percentage, she called it, for holding it for me. I figured that was fair. I wasn't hungry much anymore. I slept by the dumpster when I passed out each night. The winos were dirty, so they didn't care if I was clean. I could pee by the dumpster when I woke up. After a while, sometimes I peed when I was still asleep. Jimmy hadn't written in a long time, even though I kept writing him. But now, I was losing the letters before I finished them. The paper got all dirty in my pockets and it smelled, and I only wanted to send him pretty things from me, like he deserved.

Finally, one day, I got another letter. It had been a couple weeks since I'd checked my mail, and Ellie said she was getting real worried about me. I told her I was OK, and I tore open Jimmy's letter. It was real short. He told me they'd convicted him. They'd put him on their new fast-track system and now they said they was going to kill him. He was going to appeal, but his asshole lawyer didn't give a shit so it wasn't going to do any good. He said he loved me and it was OK if I had a new life. Would I please just send him one picture of me and the baby so he could hold it when they strapped him on the table. I started screaming. I screamed and screamed and I couldn't stop.

Ellie called the paramedics and they took me to the hospital. They gave me a bath and put me on a suicide watch. They tried to feed me, but I didn't want to eat anymore. When I started shaking, they asked me what I was taking, but all I could do was scream that those Texas bastards was going to kill my Jimmy. So after a while, they took all this blood from me. Then they put me in the drug ward and gave me AZT. Three days later, when the pains started, Ellie ran over from the shelter and held my hand. They was setting up to cut me open. The doctor wanted to do a C-section. But the baby was so small. She came too fast. One minute Ellie was helping me pant. The next she was holding me up while the doctor told me "Push, PUSH!"

Me and Jimmy's beautiful baby girl slid out, and they let me hold her, just for a minute. I was bleeding something fierce, and the baby was so tiny she had to go into an incubator. Our baby looked just like her daddy, though. She had his beautiful eyes and lots of thick curly hair and the same little dent in her chin. I begged Ellie to take a picture of the baby to send it to Jimmy. She's real persuasive, so finally the doctor told her she could. I didn't want to be in the picture, but Ellie tied her scarf around my hair quick. She took out a disposable camera she had in her purse and she told me to smile. I did. I gave my daughter a kiss and told her she was her daddy's little girl and we loved her forever. Then she was gone to the incubator. I started crying and Ellie held my hand while the doctors worked on me. Then they put a mask on my face and the last thing I remember is the doctor telling the cops that they'd damn well have to wait to talk to me.

They sent me to a drug rehab program from the hospital. Ellie arranged it, partly because it was taking me so long to heal from the surgery. I didn't much care. Something inside me had busted from the bleeding, so I wasn't going to be having any more babies. When I walked away a couple months later, Social Services had already taken my beautiful baby girl. Triola had lied to me. The drug *did* hurt Jasmine. It hurt her bad. She was born addicted and she had to go through withdrawal, even worse than I did, because she was just a baby. I was so pissed at the drugs, and I felt so bad for hurting Jasmine. I didn't want her to think her mama would hurt her ever, not ever.

Social Services said if I didn't sign the adoption papers, they'd put Jasmine in foster care until either I got my act together enough to take care of her or I screwed up so bad they could terminate my parental rights, or until I died. I didn't want her to grow up like that, floating around like me and Jimmy done after his mama died and my daddy run off. Ellie helped me get the papers fixed up real good so Jasmine would go right away to a new mama and daddy who could take care of her while she was growing up, the way me and Jimmy had always wanted for our kids. I signed the papers, but I said I wanted her always named Jasmine, because that was so pretty and it sounded kind of like Jimmy.

Ellie wanted to give me the picture she'd taken, but I told her no. I told her to send it to Jimmy, so he'd have a chance to meet his baby. I'd carried Jasmine under my heart for a long time, so I'd always remember her, even without a picture, just like I remembered my Jimmy. I asked her to write Jimmy for me and tell him I'd died having the baby. I told her to tell him I loved him and that when he got to heaven, I'd be there waiting for him, with a big smile on my face. Ellie said that was a dumb plan. She said I could make a new life for myself, that I had a lot going for me, and maybe Jimmy's appeals would work. Appeals took a long time, years and years, even on the fast track. Even in Texas, they were sometimes fair and they might say Jimmy's lawyer shouldn't have been asleep.

I smiled and told her of course she was right, and I'd keep working toward a better future. I don't think she believed me even then. But she finally agreed to write Jimmy and send him the picture and tell him I hadn't made it through the delivery, which wasn't quite the same as saying I'd died, but it wasn't really a lie. I hugged her goodbye and told her she was my friend and that I thanked her with all my heart.

Then I went back to working with Triola. She said she was sorry the stuff had hurt the baby. Her dealer had told her it was safe. Triola's not real smart, not that way, but she'd took care of me as best she could. To make it up, she shared the stuff she had with me now. Even though I could hustle the better customers again, it didn't hurt so much when I didn't have to think about Jasmine and Jimmy being gone.

Ellie told me it was really important to use rubbers now "with my partners," so that I didn't infect anyone else. She said I had HIV and I had to promise her I'd take my pills from the clinic exactly the way they told me to. Ellie'd been good to me and I didn't want to hurt anybody, so I took my pills and I mostly used rubbers, unless the johns really didn't want to. If they insisted, I figured they knew the score, and it didn't matter for me. I just got lost in Triola's stuff and spread my legs and pretended I was with my Jimmy again. But now I used it real careful. I kept myself clean and pretty enough to make money and I made sure I didn't get busted too often. I was starting to put money by again, tucking it in another little Altoids box. I kept this one in a fake heel in my shoe, though. Whenever I got five twenties extra, I traded up at the check cashing place for a hundred, so the box wouldn't get too full.

I was saving up. I knew it would take me four or five years, but that was OK. Each time I went by Ellie's, she checked her e-mail and the Internet about Texas. I tapped my heel and tried not to cry each time she told me Jimmy's asshole lawyer had lost another appeal. The last time, when those bastards in Washington, D.C., turned him down, we knew it was over. Ellie hugged me and tried to cheer me up, I was crying so hard. She told me she'd checked with her connections and Jasmine was doing fine. She'd even started kindergarten, in a pretty new dress. Even though I was still crying, I smiled for real. I was so proud. I knew my Jimmy would be so proud of his little girl. I hugged Ellie one last time and then I went back to work. Triola and I shared the corner now. After she got knifed last summer, she couldn't get as many tricks, and she felt better when I was around. I paid her for my stuff now, and I pretended I didn't notice she was ripping me off. I was still putting money by.

I was saving for tonight. Those Texas bastards are killing my Jimmy tonight. This time, I didn't go through Triola. I tucked a hundred in her purse, so she'd find it later. But I took the rest across town. I went to a dealer Triola knew and I scored some pure white powder. I told him I didn't want stuff like you put in a pipe. I wanted the junk like rich people put up their nose, but before they cut it. He thought that was real funny. When he saw I didn't want enough to deal it, just to use, he took my money and gave me a little bag of real special stuff. He told me to be sure to cut it real good, especially if I was sharing it with Triola, because she was a friend of his. I laughed back and told him not to worry. I'd be real careful.

After that, I bought some fancy new clothes, nice ones, like Jimmy used to like to see me in, and I had my hair done and my nails. I put on some good perfume, little dabs on my wrists and elbows and behind my knees and between my boobs and where my thighs meet my body. I got me a pack of the expensive rubbers, not like the kind the free clinic gives out. Then I rented a classy hotel room with flowers in the vase and a big window that opened out on the city. I opened the curtain, so anybody who wanted to watch, could. I kept out enough money for a coupla drinks and a tip for the maid. I stuffed the rest in an envelope and mailed it to Ellie as a donation in Jasmine's name. Then I went looking for the best trick I could find.

I wasn't looking for a cute guy. I was looking for some-body nice, like Jimmy. So I went to the hotel bar and said I was in town for a convention and I'd just closed a big deal and did anybody want to party with me tonight. I'd taken just enough of Triola's stuff earlier to take the edge off the wanting, so I could laugh and tell jokes. Eventually, this guy in a suit and tie like Jimmy would have wore if he'd scored came up and put his hand on my knee. He said his name was Sam and he'd like to party with a pretty girl like me. His hand was warm and strong and he smelled good, like soap and sweat, like Jimmy used to. So we went up to my room and I undressed him. I teased him and we laughed, just the way me and Jimmy used to. It was almost getting late, almost the time they were going to kill my Jimmy back in Texas. So I peeled off my dress. I even kind of blushed for real when Sam whistled and told me I was kind of thin, but I was real pretty, and he liked my perfume. Then he hugged me, and his arms were warm and alive, like Jimmy's were, so long ago. I got out the rubbers and I told him he had to be sure to use one, because everybody had to be safe these days. He laughed and said he'd want everybody to be safe with a sweet girl like me. I felt tears in my eyes, because it felt so good to hear somebody say nice things to me again.

Then Sam put his hands on my boobs, and we fell down on the bed. I'd put the powder under the pillow. I let him fuck me for a bit, to get himself going. Jimmy always liked to do that, and Sam was so nice that I actually got a little bit wet for him. Then I asked him to fuck me from behind. When he was resituating, I opened the little plastic bag and quick took out the soda straw I stole from the bar earlier and cut way down. I put the straw to my nose, and I inhaled. I sucked it all in, pure and white and powdery soft heaven.

My head exploded. Sam slid back into me and I bucked up, screaming. He asked did he hurt me, and I said, no, oh, no, it just felt so good. I ground against him, clenching my cunt muscles and fucking him as hard as I could. I didn't touch my clit. I didn't have to. My body was exploding and Sam fucked into me so hard I was coming and coming and I couldn't stop. Suddenly Jimmy was inside me. He was fucking me until I screamed and calling me his pretty girl and telling me he loved me. I heard Sam calling me, but I didn't care anymore. I had my Jimmy back. He was in me, and I was shaking and he was spurting up my cunt. He was coming and I was coming and I could feel him in me, in *me,* not just my cunt. My ears felt like they were exploding, like they were as hot as the white light screaming through my heart. And for the first time in so very, very long, I heard my Jimmy laughing.

"Come with me, sweet girl. We're going home."

I leaned into him, and we was home.

# Greek Fever

## Anne Tourney

There weren't many men in my Bible Belt town who practiced Greek love. One of the few was my father, Simon. Another was Gabriel, who was posing as our live-in handyman. My father believed that Gabriel, with his charmed hands and cock, could fix anything from a sinking roof to a rusted libido. I didn't believe anything about Gabriel except for one promise he made to me. And that was only because I had wrestled my lust into something resembling faith.

Simon and I both had Greek fever that summer. We staggered around with Greece on the brain, the light of Athens burning our bodies from inside. But while Simon retreated into his fever like a trance, I was planning to act on my affliction.

My father didn't know that I was going to Greece with his lover.

Gabriel told me what to pack: only enough clothes for sunbathing, drinking, and fucking. We could have done all those things in Oklahoma, but in Greece, Gabriel said, you could turn a life of lazy horniness into a personal philosophy. In the town of Pawsupsnatch (pop. 3,007) that kind of slutty behavior was just another reason for people to gossip about you.

The gossip would have turned into mass hysteria if the citizens of Pawsupsnatch had known what went on in our house. On my days off, Gabriel fucked me. Nights, he made love with my father. In the darkness, soft groans would drift from Simon's locked bedroom. During the day Gabriel and I would tear the house apart as we banged our way from room to room, knocking over furniture and denting the walls. Terrified of the Baptists who ran our local drugstore, I made secret trips to Tulsa to buy condoms by the trunkload. Considering Simon's social status as a widowed high school teacher, I assumed he was doing some smuggling himself. After twelve years of exile, the specter of sex had swooped back into our home, and that specter was pissed-off and ravenous.

"It's your turn, Aggie," Gabriel would murmur, starting things off with moth-wing kisses on the nape of my neck. His lips would buzz my ears while his arms roped my waist from behind. I'd burrow back into the muscular cradle of his torso until I felt his cock rise against my ass cheeks. I started wearing short, flimsy skirts so that he could get to my pussy with his fingers, cock, or tongue whenever the urge seized us. Betraying my father felt like stepping barefoot on a rusty tin can—agonizing and thrilling and toxic—but I couldn't help myself. When I came with Gabriel, mighty spasms cored my body, leaving me raving and senseless. I didn't have orgasms; I had seizures.

"I could fall in love with you in Greece," Gabriel once told me. Now that summer's long gone, I know he must have told my father the same thing.

At first I couldn't stand to hear Gabriel and Simon making love. My father's celibacy was a given, part of the deal we made when I put my life in deep-freeze so that I could look after him and his feeble heart. I knew he fell in love now and then, and that since my mother died he'd given up the struggle to love women. I must have known that his abstract love for men could translate into sex. I just never thought it would happen in my mother's bed.

My mother and father had always been discreet in their passion. As a child I never wondered how they made love, but whether they "did it" at all. At the age of twenty-eight, I wasn't prepared for this variation on the primal scene: my father having sex—intense, audible sex—with another man. My mind reeled. I wrote down a list of words to describe what two naked men might get up to, then I repeated those words until they lost their mystery. *Fellatio, sodomy, cornholing, cocksucking.* The throaty male voices taunted me, their moans melting and swirling like butter and bittersweet chocolate. Rituals went on behind that door that I couldn't visualize. Did they kiss with open lips and tongues? Did they rub their erections together, like two scouts trying to start a fire with a pair of sticks? Did they suck each other's cock with juicy abandon as they lay coiled in bed, each lover's heart thumping against the other's belly? Did they mount each other, penetrate and thrust?

From the shouts and pleas that rang through the house at night, I imagined they did all that and then some.

After Gabriel had been with us for a week, my fascination took on a harder edge. In my sexual starvation, I hallucinated that Gabriel was moving on top of me, and that the moans echoing through the walls came from my own lips, not my father's. My body ignored all taboos and began responding to the urgent sounds. My fingers stabbed my cunt in time to the squeaking bedsprings. I imagined Gabriel's mouth on my pussy, my mouth on his prick, our hands roving over each other's sweat-slick skin. In the daylight, I was mortified by the idea of being aroused by my father's lovemaking. But as I witnessed Simon's growing joy, I realized that the man sharing a bed with Gabriel was no longer just my father. With Gabriel, Simon was transformed into the man he was meant to be.

That's when I let myself start wanting Gabriel. I not only wanted him, I deserved him.

He came to us in June. Tornado weather—the sky was swollen with its own miserable promise. The air in the house felt as dead as dough that won't rise. Simon and I were reading on the front porch.

As soon as Gabriel stopped his battered Dodge and stepped out, my father and I were lost. We gaped as he strolled around the car, his hips rolling in frayed blue jeans. The tips of his savannah-blond hair were painted with sweat. His white cotton T-shirt sucked lovingly at his damp chest. A halo of black gnats circled his face and throat. Suddenly I wanted more than anything to be one of those miniscule insects, sipping at that man's juice, stinging, biting, living a flash of a life in the warmth of his body.

"Morning," he said. "Need any odd jobs done around here?" His voice was like his looks: bronzed, sun-creased, lubed with honey. In the bilious daylight his eyes were snake green.

Odd jobs? In a household consisting of a lonely, horny librarian; her lonelier, hornier father; and about three thousand books (half of them written in dead languages), I'd say there were a few odd jobs to be done. Yes, sir.

My father rose and walked down the front steps. Gabriel extended his hand (God, to think where that hand would end up that summer), and my father clutched it for what seemed like forever.

"I think we could find you some work," Simon said.

Gabriel stayed for lunch. I prepared the food while my father and Gabriel got to know each other. As I carried the plates to the table, my father announced, "Gabriel just got back from Athens. Agatha, he lived there for a *year*. He speaks a bit of the *language*."

Around here, that just about made him Plato reincarnate.

Simon's face was a searchlight, casting its beam back and forth between me and Gabriel, but resting mostly on Gabriel. Barring death or disaster, there was no way this stranger was going to leave our house.

And he didn't. The first night, Gabriel made a nest for himself on our sofa. Early the next morning, while he was taking a shower, I went through his belongings. I found a few dirty socks and T-shirts and a wallet with nothing but seven dollars inside: no credit cards, no driver's license. I held a shirt up to my nose and inhaled his smell, as dizzying as a stag's musk.

The water stopped running. I flung Gabriel's things back into a heap. I thought he would appear any second, padding barefoot into the living room. His brown body would be sparkling with moisture, his hair slicked back, water clinging to his nipples and welling out of his navel and trickling down through the dark-gold tendrils that fanned his pubis.

From upstairs I heard voices: masculine, companionable, an intimate rumbling.

Love banter.

I buried my hand in the heap of quilts and felt no trace of warmth. Gabriel hadn't slept on this sofa; he'd slept in my father's bed. While I was trying to find out whether Gabriel was a traveling axe murderer, he and Simon had been showering together.

Over the nights that followed, as I lay in my bed listening to the ongoing seduction of my father, I developed a theory about Gabriel. I decided that Gabriel wasn't a man or a god, but a spirit who goes back and forth between the worlds, like the *daimon* of Greek myth. This spirit came over from Athens in some tourist's shopping bag, landed in the Bible Belt, and answered the cry for love that came from Simon and me. I never thought to analyze Gabriel's sexual preferences: whether he was gay, straight, or some hybrid of the two. From the first time I saw him, I knew that Gabriel could take on any shape you wanted.

Since my mother's death Simon had fallen in love a few times, but until Gabriel, his loves were always wildly suppressed and embarrassing, like the crumb that gets stuck in your throat in a fancy restaurant. Simon had a disturbing tendency to fall for his students. He taught history and driver's ed at the high school, but long ago he had earned a Ph.D. in classics, and he missed Ancient Greek with a pain that showed in his eyes. Every so often a male student would sidle up to him and confess that he wanted to read Sappho or Plato or Aristophanes in the original. Boom—Simon would be gone. He couldn't help it; Greek was the language he loved with.

This whole affair would have been easier if Gabriel had been one of my father's pupils, and my father had suffered with love for years, waiting for an illicit yearning to ripen into a legitimate romance when Gabriel came of age.

Nothing in our lives was ever that easy.

The first words Gabriel said to me outside of Simon's earshot were "I love girls your age." The way he let the word "love" shimmy down his tongue, it sounded more like he wanted to say "crave."

It was late at night. Somehow, under the dense shelf of heat that had been building up all day, Simon had managed to fall asleep. Gabriel and I sat outside at the picnic table.

"How old do you think I am?"

"Stand up."

I stood.

Though I couldn't see Gabriel's eyes, I could feel him looking me up and down. My nipples stuck straight out and begged his eyes to linger.

"Eighteen?"

"I'm older than I look," I warned.

I wasn't about to admit that I was twenty-eight. My personal fashion profile hadn't changed much since I was sixteen, the year my mother died.

"Take off that top, and I could make a better guess."

I could sense Gabriel grinning in the darkness. He wasn't wearing a shirt himself. All day he'd worn nothing but a pair of cut-offs, so short that I could practically hear his balls chafing against the ragged hems. Spit crackled in my parched mouth.

"I'll take off my top if you answer a question," I said.

"What kind of question?"

"Does it matter?"

"Sure. If it's about the past, I won't answer it. And if it's about the future, I can't."

"Do you love Simon?"

Gabriel didn't answer. I longed to sit down again, to get back to the promising buzz that had risen between us. But I had to keep standing there, like a prosecutor waiting for testimony.

Then Gabriel asked me a question.

"Have you ever been to Greece?"

"No. I've never been anywhere."

"How come?"

I sat down again. "My father has heart trouble, so I've stayed close to home. After high school I got a job at the public library, and I've been there ever since."

When it came to life, I was a virgin in all but the old cock-in-the-hole sense. Hand me any book, and I could catalog it even in a coma. I could find answers to questions about everything from ant hills to transvestitism, but I sometimes woke up in the middle of the night, my heart galloping, and realized that I might die before I ever experienced cunnilingus.

"You should go to Greece, Aggie. You'd see things differently there. Simon knows what I mean."

"My father's never been to Greece, either."

"Even so, he understands me. He knows what I am."

"Do you think you might fall in love with him?"

Gabriel laughed. "I told you I couldn't answer questions about the future."

"If you don't love him, why are you here?"

"I like the way he stares at me when I'm naked. I like the way he touches me. And because I'm dead broke and he's letting me stay here for free."

I should have hated Gabriel for admitting that, but I didn't. I could see him in Greece, sunbathing naked in the rubble of a ruined temple, recharging his body in the light of an amoral sun. I could see myself there, too, emptied of everything but a desire for life. Free of taking care of Simon. Free of being Agatha.

"I want to go to Greece," I said.

"Me too. But I can't get there without any money."

"I have money."

"Sure, Aggie."

"I do! Not a fortune, but enough."

"Then we'll go," Gabriel said.

I believed him.

"You promise?"

"I promise," Gabriel said. "We'll go."

"When?"

"Whenever you're ready."

I didn't decide that night. I did my research, throttled my conscience, and decided we'd leave in September. By the time my father started the new school year, Gabriel and I would be in Athens. From there we'd travel to the islands whose names I murmured in my bed at night like incantations.

It started on a Monday morning. Simon was teaching summer school. Gabriel was mowing the lawn. I stood at the kitchen sink, sipping a glass of iced coffee and inhaling the fragrance of cut grass. I should have known something was up when the lawnmower's drone stopped.

"Aggie?"

I hadn't heard Gabriel enter the kitchen. Coffee spilled down my chin. The glass fell from my hand and shattered on the floor.

"Shit!" I grabbed a dishcloth.

Gabriel was on his knees, picking up the shards of glass. I knelt beside him. A ruby bead welled out of the pad of his thumb. I grabbed his hand and stuck his thumb in my mouth.

His thumb tasted of gasoline, grass, and the dangerous tang of blood. I closed my eyes and sucked at the digit as if it were a straw to his soul. I sucked greedily, drinking his experiences, his memories, the mysteries of his past. I didn't consider what I was doing until I opened my eyes and found him staring at me. His eyes were a clear, steady gold that morning. I could almost believe he was sincere when he said, "I could fall in love with you in Greece."

"I don't know if I could fall in love with you," I said, "but I sure as hell need to fuck you."

We stampeded upstairs like wild horses, tripping over each other to get to my bedroom, where we undressed in a mute frenzy. Naked, we slowed down for some sensual investigation. His skin was moist from working outdoors; my fingertips clung softly wherever they made contact. He cupped my breasts and suckled my nipples until I thought I'd cry from the keen joy. His hard-on nudged my thigh, but he wasn't in any rush to enter me. Instead he moved down, spangling my belly with kisses. A prayer took shape in my mind.

*Oh, Lord, let him eat my pussy.*

*Oh, Lord, let this be better than that time in the truck with Hank Maples.*

Then Gabriel was turning my cunt inside out like the cuff of a velvet sleeve, and his tongue was wandering through grooves I didn't know I had, places that hadn't been touched by anything more exotic than a washcloth. Gabriel's mouth had more tricks than a whole herd of circus ponies, and that morning he showed me all of them. The flutter. The clit-flicker. The figure eight, the labial lunge, the lick-out-the-slipper, the toad-in-the-hole. He licked me into a state I've only heard drug addicts talk about: a mindless, floating ecstasy.

The floating got turbulent when he started to suck on my clit. He slid one finger inside me, then two, then three, then an impossible four. Deeper his hand plunged. My body felt paralyzed from the waist down, except for the red zone between my thighs. I was wetter than I'd ever known a woman could be, until I hit my peak and unleashed a flood. My body arched so high that I could swear I saw Greece. While Gabriel rode me to his own climax, I watched a delirious light dance against a blinding blue sky.

After he fell asleep I explored him, inch by inch. Gabriel's skin was a map. His tan formed continents of bronze and seas of dusky rose. It was not the kind of tan you get working in an oil field or fishing for crappie. His body bore the imprint of ancient light.

But Gabriel wasn't interested in ancient light. He was more concerned with drinking beer and scamming free plane tickets and screwing outdoors. Yet in that sense, Simon would have said, he was as ancient as they come: the living, breathing soul of unreasoning desire.

As a teenager I'd read my father's copy of Plato's *Symposium*. Simon worshipped those dialogues; he'd have given his life to go back to ancient Athens and sit in on that dinner party with Socrates and his friends, drinking and laughing and talking about love. I didn't know what I was looking for in that book. Possibly a balm for the uneasiness I felt about my parents' marriage, or a map to the places Simon traveled in his mind when his body seemed so restless.

When I read what Diotima told Socrates about love and procreation, my heart turned into a sack of wet cement. Love is creative, she said; it strives for immortality in different forms. A person can create with his body—have children with women, in other words—or reach for a more exalted love and produce children of the soul. It's the second kind of love that takes you from the physical to the spiritual plane, and finally earns you a ticket to absolute beauty. I figured that second kind of love was what Simon secretly craved, what kept him awake at night, incapable of resting in my mother's bed.

I once asked my mother how she and Simon fell in love. She told me, for the hundredth time, the story of how they met. He was a graduate student in classics, she was an English major who wrote poetry, both believed secretly in fate. Once they realized that they not only shared a passion for Plato, but had been raised in the same stultifying town, they started to see the handprints of destiny everywhere they looked. That same destiny brought me into being before they were married, and between my mother's longing for respectability and my insistent need to be fed, they went back to Pawsupsnatch to take reliable jobs at the high school and public library.

But that wasn't the information I wanted. I wanted a bulletin from the world of adult love, some succinct secret to the mystery of passion.

My mother took a long time to think about this. "In the beginning," she finally said, "we thought we were two halves of the same whole. Later we realized that we simply loved the same books. And we loved you, of course."

"You mean that was *enough?*" I squealed.

My mother looked at me, bemused. "Books and a child turned out to be plenty for me," she said.

When I was sixteen, my mother died of ovarian cancer. In some dirty nook of his conscience, I think Simon saw her death as the ultimate sign that he'd failed at love. Twelve years later Gabriel came along. My father didn't seem to care who he was, or what he wanted; he just clung to Gabriel's body as if it were the last lifeboat on a desolate sea.

Maybe Simon thought that at some point down the road, he would see absolute beauty through a drifter with hazel eyes and a brass ass.

The last week of August I made dinner for Simon and Gabriel every night. Guilt stripped my appetite, but it made me want to cook like crazy. The china rattled in my hands as I set out the plates.

"Are you all right, Agatha?" Simon asked.

I saw something besides concern in my father's face—a plea, or a challenge: *Don't take him away from me,* or *Go ahead and try.*

"The catfish is terrific, Aggie."

Gabriel stuffed a forkful of fish into his mouth. He winked at me. I scowled and fussed with the napkin in my lap. An angry red lovebite marked the inside of my thigh. I had been coming when Gabriel gave me that bite. He had five fingers curved up inside my cunt like a funnel when he bit me in the softest part of my leg, and I went over the edge.

"Nothing like catfish fresh from the lake," my father said.

We had bought the filets at Shop n' Save. Every time I lifted my fork I could smell Gabriel's musk on my hand.

That afternoon Gabriel had stolen a rowboat from the dock of someone's summer cabin, and we had rowed out to the middle of the water. We had told Simon we were going fishing, but the only pole that came out on that expedition was about eight inches long.

We sprawled in the boat, our legs intertwined, and rubbed suntan lotion into each other's skin. If anyone had been watching, they might have wondered why we applied lotion mainly to the parts of our bodies that were covered by clothes. The ruddy head of his erection was nosing its way up through the waistband of his shorts, and the seat of my skirt was slippery with my arousal. My cunt must have known, even if my brain didn't, that life was going to take a peculiar turn in the next week. How else can I explain why I ordered Gabriel to eat me right there in the boat, instead of dragging him over to the sheltering trees along the lake's shore?

He grinned. "You don't care if we attract an audience?"

I growled, spread my thighs, and pushed him down.

Leaning back, I closed my eyes against the sun. Under the tent of my skirt, Gabriel's head bobbed as he tongued me. The boat rocked crazily, shivering with the pounding of my pulse.

"You've never been this turned on," Gabriel said, his voice muffled. "You're soaking wet."

"Shut up. That tongue wasn't made for talking."

But he was right; I'd never felt such a primitive, unself-conscious lust. The rude midday sun blessed us, the sexy *waa-waa* of the insect chorus mocked my sense of propriety, and I felt as if the gods of desire were urging us on. I hooked a leg under Gabriel's thigh and applied a steady friction to his crotch. His cock, still trapped in denim, was a hot, dry bulge against my shin. Suddenly he groaned and pulled back. His spine arched. His body trembled. He bit down hard on my thigh as he thrust against my leg, spilling come onto the floor of the boat. I stared up into the sun as I climaxed, watching the light pulsate with my cunt's throb, knowing I could be bat-blind when it was over but not caring if I lost my sight.

Needless to say, the boat capsized. We had to slosh around the Shop n' Save like drowned rats to find our dinner.

If I'd known that would be the last time Gabriel made me come, I would have made him eat me till his jaw locked. I would have made him lick my pussy till his tongue bled.

Two days before we were supposed to go to Greece, I decided to leave work early and go home. I don't know why. I'd never had a premonition before, and I'd rather not have one again.

I found Gabriel crouched on the floor beside my bed. The mattress had been pushed back. His fingers shuttled rapidly; for a second I thought he was saying the rosary. But it wasn't beads he was handling; it was my money. I kept a cash hoard under my mattress, in case the bank ever got hit by a tornado.

Gabriel looked up.

"What are you doing?"

"Getting ready for our trip."

"Bullshit."

Gabriel clambered to his feet. His backpack dangled from one shoulder.

"Leaving already?"

"Yep."

"Without me?"

He sighed.

"Have you really been to Greece?"

"Sure," he said.

But I knew that even if he was telling the truth, Gabriel hadn't been to the Greece he'd promised me. He'd been to a scorched, sweaty place, crowded with disappointed tourists who couldn't find the Greece they'd imagined, either.

"Get out of here," I said. "Take the money and get out."

It took every ounce of willpower I had to say that. A rabid animal was clawing at my gut, frantic with need. Then there was Simon. I didn't even want to think about my father's fragile heart.

Gabriel let his backpack slide off his shoulder. I knew what was coming. He walked up to me, standing so close that his chest grazed my nipples. Wary as an animal tamer, he circled me with his arms, then let his hands settle on my waist. Through the fabric of my skirt his thumbs hooked my panties and slid them down. They slithered to the floor like something small and valueless drifting into murky water.

"One more time, Aggie," he said. "Let me fuck you one more time."

I unbuttoned his fly and pulled out his cock. He was already fully erect, as if my pain had turned him on. I didn't want that sorcerer's wand anywhere close to my core. I knelt and took him in my mouth. No seduction, no ceremony, just a hard, angry suck, the kind of release he might get from a stranger in a public restroom. I gripped the root of his shaft with one hand and tugged with my lips, letting my teeth scrape his skin. He yelped; I dragged harder. His body tensed.

I usually didn't swallow, but today I wasn't about to stop. I gripped his ass and drew him deeper than I'd ever taken him, so deep that I almost choked. For a moment he was absolutely still, then he bucked and yelled. I let him shoot his bitter sap down my throat, knowing it wasn't safe, but needing to memorize the flavor of his particular evil.

"I'll never forget the way you taste," I said when I had caught my breath. "You taste like a lie. Now get out."

Leaving, Gabriel didn't make a sound. I felt him depart, though. The *daimon*. The spirit who comes and goes between worlds.

After Gabriel left, I took a walk. I ended up walking all the way out to the lake where Gabriel and I had made love. I conjured my father's face in the water and rehearsed what I would say.
*Gabriel's gone.*

*No, Daddy—*

*He's not coming back.*

My father would know we were heading for an emotional shitstorm if I called him "Daddy." He'd been "Simon" to me since my mother's funeral.

When I got home, the house was dark. Simon must have found out already. He was probably halfway to Texas by now, driving madly through the darkness, searching the highway for Gabriel's Dodge.

All night I waited. As soon as a respectable wedge of sunrise appeared, I called the high school principal at home.

"Simon's gone," I announced, too tired to be frantic anymore. "I'm going to need help finding him."

"Finding him? What for?"

"You mean you know where he is?"

"Why, Simon got on a plane to Athens yesterday! Took a leave of absence so he could travel in Greece. Big dream of his. I wasn't thrilled at the short notice, but with his heart, you know...Agatha?" The principal's voice rose to a dumfounded squeal. "Where the heck have you been?"

Agatha?

Was that me?

Where *had* I been? So fuck-drunk that the town gossip hadn't reached me. Once I landed at the bottom of my shock, I looked around and saw sense in the depths. My father and I had a hard time with love, but we were even worse at dealing with pain. Of *course* Simon hadn't told me he was leaving. I'd never planned to tell him about my escape, either. We'd both gotten passports, purchased tickets. The only difference was that Simon got away first.

*I could fall in love with you in Greece.*

Father or daughter—the object of lust hardly mattered to Gabriel, who could pound everything sacred to a pulp with his magic cock.

This is the way I justified my father's flight, after I'd talked things over with the Simon who occupies my head. If Simon hadn't gone to Greece with Gabriel, he would have gone alone. But his destination would have been a Greece of his own making, and you wouldn't see him in this world again. He'd be having dinner in some Athens of his mind, a world of immortal light. Every once in a while, a nurse would come by with a pleated paper cup and order him to swallow some pills.

Blood is thicker than water, yes. But you don't crave a glass of blood when you're dying of thirst.

Hell, I hope Simon earned his ticket to absolute beauty, grabbed Gabriel's cock, and took that gorgeous bastard with him. I have no idea where Gabriel is, but in my optimistic moments I imagine he's still with Simon, drinking retsina at some taverna by the sea and listening to my father weave his own theory of love.

# Shoes

*Kate Bachus*

I married him because of his name. I liked the sound of it;
I still do. Now we are carefully close. We are eggshell roman-
tics. We treat our love as if it is something ephemeral and
fragile, and that strikes me as wrong somehow, if I allow
myself to think about it at all.

The shoes that I wear to work are like the marriage has
become. They are not comfortable, but I pride myself on how
well I function in them.

Today I bought six pairs of shoes. Two are identical, but
they are perfect, and I don't want to run the risk of damaging
or losing a pair once I come to rely heavily on them, once they
have become an essential part of my wardrobe.

Aman accompanies me on my shoe-buying trip. He is an
old friend whom I am surprised to find still with me, when I
think about how much I have changed over the years. We are
like two cats in the same house, aloof and comfortable. From
where he sits without a trace of impatience in one of the boutique's shantung chairs, he tells me that he hates a pair of
black loafers I've tried on.

"A cut heel has no place on that shoe," he says, "and it looks plastic."

We still manage to spend four hundred dollars on shoes, or rather, I do, and then we have lunch.

I do not understand or like Aman's wife, nor do I try. He married three years after I did, and seems complacently happy. I cannot comprehend it. Aman wears suits handmade from Egyptian silk, in colors I would never conceive of for a man: deep sage green, or rich mustard gold. His wedding band looks like a signet ring on his narrow finger; I think he is the closest I will ever come to knowing royalty.

During lunch, in a rotunda surrounded by ferns, overlooking rows and rows of designer gowns and minks, I tell him I need a pair of blue sling-backs, preferably nubuck. Aman puts down his coffee cup and says that I've copped out.

"What?"

"Copped out," he says with his usual genteel enunciation. "You are stuck at two inches. Maybe two and a half. You are paralyzed in your reluctance to go any higher, and it's a shame. Your calves beg for more."

The waiter comes and goes and we engage in a polite and purely ritual haggle over the check before I ask, "What?" again.

I have, as I think about it, the clear sense that anything over three inches is trashy and antifeminist. Anything under an inch and a half is frowsy.

Outside the galleria, Aman arrests a cab with a restrained gesture and opens the door for me.

"I thought you liked my shoes," I say in the cab.

"I *approve* of your shoes," he says. I fail to see the difference.

At work the next day I call Aman. Our friendship remains strictly eight-to-five because of his wife. But since it feels like an emergency, I call him on his cell phone as he is on his way home.

"You're wrong, Aman. You of all people; it's about good taste." It sounds accusatory at best and shrill at worst. There is a long pause before he replies.

"I think you've mistaken context for identity," he says, and either goes out of range or hangs up on me.

That night I ask my husband what he thinks of my shoes. We are sitting in the living room, and he turns and looks at me as if I have caught him at something he wishes I hadn't. He looks reflexively at my feet, which are bare, and I explain quickly "in general," and then I can tell he has even less of an idea of how to respond.

Later on, in bed, he tells me that he likes my shoes, that they are classy and that I have good taste. But by that time, of course, it's too late. We laugh about it and I reassure him and stifle my anger at his relieved willingness to let it go.

The next day at work I look in the yellow pages under "shoes." By the time I have found the place I think I want, I have almost talked myself out of going there. Then I rationalize that women should take responsibility for their own self-statement; that gets me down the curb and into a cab.

When I call Aman from the cab and he tells me he has meetings, I take great pleasure in hanging up on him.

The shop does not tuck its dressing rooms behind large racks of clearance and postseason clothes. Instead I am led onto a sort of stage, off of which open the dressing room doors. I realize as I look down into the shop that I am on display. I set the two pairs of shoes—ones I thought I should buy, which makes them now suspect—and try Aman again.

"Will you come down here?" I ask, and he says "of course," and I hand the shoes back to the clerk and sit on stage to wait.

"Choose for me," I tell him when he arrives. I care less than I should about my tone, which is half demand, half plea.

He looks around the shop, and after a pleasant smile to the clerk chooses a pair of the trashiest, most impossible shoes I have ever seen. They will force me practically *en pointe,* and they have small, flimsy-looking locks that dangle from the ankle straps.

I expect him to hand them to me, but he doesn't. He beckons me to the edge of the stage, where I sit with my legs dangling. Reaching down, he deftly slides off one taupe pump, and then the other. I notice his ring again, his manicured fingernails, and the size and shape of my feet in his hands.

He glances up, unsmiling, and picks up the shoes. I realize that I hate them. And yet, my foot slides easily and obediently into that impossible position, the stretch of one part answered by the curl of another. My feet are pinioned by cheap patent leather and Aman's insistent, aristocratic hands.

He buckles the strap of the shoe around my ankle, and I am wet.

He does not help me up, but rather lets me struggle, like an awkward foal in my Italian suit, until by leverage and balance I get to my feet and stand in front of him on the stage.

At that moment I regret never having had sex with him— and I find that I no longer need him.

I confront my husband that night, naked in my new shoes. At first he does what he thinks he should do: he touches me, and tells me I am intense and beautiful and full of wonderful surprises.

I tell him he is a shit, and that he is lying.

We fight. When we are done fighting he tells me I look like a whore in those shoes and I tell him, "I *feel* like a whore."

It is a terrible cliché, and we laugh and laugh.

"You are *my* whore," he says in a deep and threatening voice, and we laugh again, but when I promise to slut myself for him I mean it.

That confuses him, and I see he both does and does not

want that. Both of us are aroused and scared. Everything has ground to a halt.

Then he repeats, "You are *my* whore," as he clumsily grabs a fistful of my hair. I remember Aman's hands, and I am not sure if it is the memory or the contrast that opens me to this.

We stand like that for a moment, and I feel trapped, ludicrous, exposed. He rocks me side to side by my hair and I almost topple, almost lose my balance off those impossible shoes.

"I'm going to suck your cock," I say. I'm not sure how to behave—perhaps like the woman I was onstage in the shop. But here in the bedroom I have only the shoes for a costume. I grasp his cock through his pants, underhand. I have seen that done.

Now we stand, each of us with our arms extended: He looks down at my hand on his cock and hardens. He breathes out in a sigh, a relieved sigh.

"Stop it," I say. "Fucking stop it." I hate his relief, I hate that he will be relieved and then I will acquiesce and everything will be all right again. I think of the rows of useless, redundant shoes in my closet: Things are not all right, they are not OK at all.

I squat. I squat down in my new shoes and look at the shape his cock makes through his blue pajama bottoms. Bullshit, I think, and I yank his cock out, clench it in my fist. I suck it hard and angrily into my mouth.

"Yes," he breathes, and *no*, I think at that tone of relief of his, as his hand slackens and loosens from where he had clenched it in my hair. I suck harder, furious, as if I could somehow siphon a response, a yelp, a protest. As if I could suck out of him anything other than his fearful, relieved, and disinterested surrender.

He arches back, away from me. This is not resistance, but retreat; I seize his ass, my nails dig into his round cheeks, the flesh of his thighs.

I am suddenly aware of my own legs spread underneath me, the feel of patent leather and the imprint of the buckle pressing into my thigh. I'm aware of myself spread open over the shoes, and now I don't give a fuck anymore about his hand, which dangles at his side, which never found a new grip in my hair. I don't give a fuck about the surrendered, relieved part of him that thinks this is—that we are—OK. My tongue sweeps his skin deeply into my mouth. When he groans I squeeze my fingers tighter into his ass, and my legs burn from squatting and I am wet, far wetter than Aman had made me.

I sit down hard on the shoes, and as he comes I stop holding onto everything else, except that, except where we are, except him.

Although we have made a pact that we will never go to sleep angry, I take a blanket and carry it out into the living room and lie down on the couch in my new shoes. My husband looks at me in hurt confusion.

I pull the blanket over me. I think of the neat rows of shoes in my closet. I think of my husband. I reach down under the blanket and touch the shoes, as if they were an amulet, or a charm.

# Riding the Rails
## Sacchi Green

"Hey, Jo! Josie Benoit!" A voice from my past, fitting all too well with the setting: the Springfield train station, visible through foggy windows and blowing snow. I'd gone to college not far from here, and so had that voice's owner.

"If it isn't Miss Theresa," I grunted, and kept on tugging at the sheepskin jacket caught behind a suitcase on the overhead rack.

"I never forget an ass," Terry said pointedly, casing mine as I reached upward.

"Sure as hell wouldn't have known yours." My jacket finally yielded. I tossed it over the voluptuous décolletage of my seated companion. A few minutes earlier Yasmin had been whining about being cold. Now, of course, for a new audience, she shrugged off the covering with an enthusiasm that threatened to shrug off her low-cut silk blouse as well. Not that it had been doing much to veil her pouting nipples.

Terry, brushing snow off her shoulders and shaking it from her hair, rightly accepted my remark as a compliment. Fourteen years ago she'd been on the lumpy side; now she was buff, and all style. Sandy hair lightened, cropped, waxed just right; multiple piercings on the left ear and eyebrow, giving her face a rakish slant; studded black leather cut to make the best of the work she'd done on her body. I'd have felt mundane, with my straight black hair twisted up into a utilitarian knot and my brown uniform, not ironed all that well since Katzi had taken off—if I ever gave a damn about appearances. Which might have had something to do with why Katzi took off. Which had a whole lot to do with why I hadn't gotten laid in two months and wasn't finding it easy to resist Yasmin's efforts.

"You just get on?" Terry asked. "Didn't see you in the station. No way I could have overlooked your little friend." Her eyes raked Yasmin, who practically squirmed with delight.

"Been on since White River Junction," I said shortly. It was more than clear that Terry expected an introduction. "Yasmin, Terry O'Brian. We were in college together. Terry, Princess Yasmin, fourth wife of the Sultan of Isbani." It was some satisfaction to see Terry's jaw drop for an instant before her suave butch facade resurfaced.

"Ooh, Terry!" Yasmin warbled, jiggling provocatively. "I didn't know Sergeant Jo had such nice friends!"

"The princess somehow…missed…leaving New Hampshire with her husband's entourage," I said. "They'd been visiting her stepson at Dartmouth. I'm escorting her to D.C. to meet them." As far as I could tell, it had been a combination of Yasmin's laziness and the head wife's hatred that had culminated in her missing the limo caravan, and her absence going unnoticed until too late. I was developing a good deal of sympathy for the head wife.

"The weather's too risky for flying or driving," I added, "but the train should make it through. Not supposed to be much snow south of Connecticut."

"Well, now," Terry said, sliding into the seat facing Yasmin. "I'll be happy to share security duty as far as New York."

"Don't get too happy." I sat down beside my charge. There were suddenly more limbs between the seats than would comfortably fit; I tried to let my long legs stretch into the aisle, but that tilted my ass too close to Yasmin, who wriggled appreciatively against my holster. I straightened up. "This is official business. The last thing I need is an international incident."

I wondered why the hell I hadn't told Terry to fuck off in the first place. Did I hope she'd distract Yasmin enough to take off some of the pressure? The tension had been building all morning. Even the rhythm of the train had been driving me toward the edge, with its subtle, insistent vibration. Or maybe it was just that the little bitch was too damned good at the game and too clearly driven by spite. I don't have to like a tease to call her on it; if I hadn't been on the job I'd have given Yasmin more than she knew she was asking for, and if it left my conscience a bit scuffed, what the hell—other parts of me would have earned a fine, lingering glow.

But I was on duty, and she was doubly untouchable, and knew it. Seven more hours of this was going to be a particularly interesting version of Hell.

"Keep it professional, Jo," Lieutenant Willey had said. "This one's a real handful."

"I noticed," I'd told her. Several handfuls, in fact, in all the right places, with all the right moves. "Don't worry. I know better than to fuck the sheep I'm herding." She should have slapped me down for that, but instead she rolled her eyes toward the door, and I saw, too late, that the troublesome sheep had just come in. No chance she hadn't heard me. Anger sparked with interest sharpened her kittenish face, segueing into challenge as she looked me up and down.

"You're off to a great start," the lieutenant said dryly. "Just bear in mind that the Sultan wants her back 'untouched,' and I'd just as soon not have to argue the semantics of that with the State Department." Something in her usually impassive expression made me wonder whether our charge had come on to her. If so, I was sure sorry I'd missed it.

By the time the train crossed from Vermont into Massachusetts, I realized Yasmin would come on to any available pair of trousers, with no discrimination as to what filled them. Even the professionally affable conductor got flustered when she rubbed up against him in passing, and she had a threesome of college boys so interested that I'd made the mistake of putting a proprietary arm around her shoulders and shooting them my best dyke-cop look as I yanked her back to our seats. The look worked fine, but it encouraged Yasmin to renew her attack on me.

"Ow!" she yelped when I tightened my grip on a hand that kept going where it had no business. "Why you are so mean to Yasmin?" Her coquettish pout left me cold, but a definite heat was building where her hand had trailed over my ass and nudged between my thighs. She knew I wasn't impervious.

"Let's just stick to the business of getting you back to your husband," I said neutrally, aware of the continuing interest of the college kids three seats back. The less drama here the better.

"Why do you worry? He can't order them to cut off your balls, the way they did to Haroun just for looking."

"Right, and you can't yank me around by them, either," I muttered. The glitter of pleasurable recollection in her eyes was nauseating. What little I'd read about female genital mutilation flashed through my mind, and for a few minutes I really *was* impervious to her charms.

Terry's company, whatever the complications, might be better than being alone with Yasmin—unless my competitive instincts reared up and made it all exponentially worse.

Terry could have been reading my mind. "Gee, Jo," she said, "remember the last time you introduced me to one of your little friends?" Her grin was demonic.

"How could I forget? You healed up pretty well, though." I stared pointedly at the scar running under her pierced eyebrow.

"Nothing like a dueling scar to intrigue the ladies," Terry said cheerfully. "You seem to have found a good dentist."

"You bet." I flashed what Katzi used to call my alpha bitch grin.

Yasmin was practically frothing with excitement, jiggling her assets and leaning toward Terry to offer an in-depth view of her cleavage and a whiff of her sensuous perfume. When she balanced herself with a far-from-accidental hand high on my thigh, I realized that all I'd done was set her up to play us off against each other.

"So, Terry," I said, firmly removing the fingers trying to make their way toward my treacherously responsive crotch, "What are you up to these days? Still living in the area?"

"I'm a paralegal in Northampton," she said. "Going to law school nights." Her gaze lingered on my badge, and for a rare instant I was hyper-conscious of the breast underneath it. "Funny how we both got onto the straight side of the law."

"No kidding," I said. "I heard that anything goes in Hamp these days, but can you go to court rigged out like that?"

"I could, but I don't." I was pleasantly surprised to see a bit of a flush rise from her neck to her jaw line. "I'm on my way to New York to do a reading at a bookstore in the East Village."

"You're a writer?" My surprise was hardly flattering, and her jaw tightened, as the flush extended all the way to her hairline.

"On the side, yeah," she said brusquely. "Doesn't pay much, but the fringe benefits can be outstanding."

"Hey, I'll just bet they are, if the stories match the get-up! Erotica groupies, huh?"

Terry caught the new respect in my voice and relaxed. She let her legs splay apart. I'd already noticed she was packing; now Yasmin stared at the huge bulge stretching the black leather pants along the right thigh, and her kewpie-doll mouth formed an awe-struck "O."

"Loaded for bear, aren't we," I said. "Ah, the literary life. I'll have to check out some of your stuff—maybe get you to autograph a book." I was more than half serious. She started to grin, and then an odd, startled look swept over her face. I glanced down and saw Yasmin's stockinged foot nudging against the straining black leather.

It wasn't a big enough deal to account for my first raging impulse to break Yasmin's leg. I managed to suppress it, but by then everything seemed to be happening in slow motion. Terry's presence was definitely making things worse. Much worse.

Yasmin pulled her silk skirt up so that we could get the full benefit of the shapely leg extended between the seats and the toes caressing the leather-sheathed cock. Then she applied enough force so that Terry caught her breath and automatically shifted her hips to get the most benefit; I felt the pressure as if she were prodding my own clit. But all I was packing was a gun, and that was on my hip.

I know from experience that you don't get the optimum angle the way Yasmin was working. But you can get damned close. Katzi used to tease me like that in restaurants, her leg up under the table, her foot in my lap, her eyes gleaming wickedly as she watched me struggle not to make the kind of sounds you can't make in public. She knew I wouldn't let myself come, because I just can't manage it without making a lot of noise.

The train wasn't crowded, but it was public. Terry's head was thrown back, her eyes glazing over, her hands gripping the seat. I was afraid my breathing was even louder than hers, and damned sure my cunt was just as hot. I had to stop the little bitch, but I was afraid if I touched her I'd do serious damage.

Then Yasmin, with a sly sidelong glance at me, unbuttoned her blouse and spread it open. As she fondled her breasts, her rosy nipples, which had thrust against the silky fabric all morning as though permanently engorged, grew even fuller and harder. Her torso undulated as her butt squirmed against the seat. Her foot was still working Terry's equipment, but her focus had shifted.

"God *damn!*" whispered Terry. Or maybe it was me. Yasmin turned slightly and leaned toward me, still working her flesh, offering it to me, watching my reaction with half-closed eyes, her little pink tongue moving over her full upper lip. The tantalizing effect of her perfume was magnified by the musk of three aroused bodies.

"We're coming into Hartford." Terry's strangled words sounded far away. "We'll be at the station any minute!"

Yasmin's voice, soft, taunting, so close that I felt her breath on my throat, echoed through my head. "Sergeant Jo doesn't have the balls to fuck a sheep!"

I snapped.

I lunged.

With my right hand I clamped her wrists together above her head. With my left arm across her windpipe I pinned her to the seat back, I leaned over her, one knee between her thighs. Then I dropped my hands to her shoulders and shook her so hard that her head bobbled and her tits jiggled against my shirt front and the hard edges of my badge.

A strong hand grabbed my shoulder and yanked me back. When I resisted, something whacked me fairly hard across the back of my head. Then a soft, bulky object—my sheepskin jacket—was shoved down between us.

"Damnit, Jo, cool it!" Terry hissed. "And you," she said to Yasmin in a tone slightly less harsh, "you little slut—and I mean that, of course, in the best possible sense of the word—cover up or I'll let the sergeant toss you out onto the train platform."

I nearly turned on her, but people were moving down the aisles to get off the train, and more people would be getting on. By the time the train was rolling again, I'd begun to get a grip, although I was still breathing hard, and my heart, along with several other body parts, was still pounding.

"Thanks," I muttered. "I guess I needed that."

"What you need," Terry said deliberately, "is a good fucking. Jesus, Jo, if you don't get it off pretty soon, you'll have not only your international incident, but the mother of all lawsuits!"

She was right. I glanced at Yasmin. She had stopped whimpering and sat clutching my jacket around herself, watching us with great interest.

I pushed myself up into the aisle. "Can I trust you to keep her out of trouble for a couple of minutes while I at least take a leak?"

"You can count on me," Terry said, and I had to go with it.

There was a handicapped-accessible restroom just across from us, long and roomy by Amtrak standards. I pissed, tied my long straggling hair back up as well as I could with a mirror too low to show anything above my chin, and leaned my pelvis against the rounded edge of the sink. It was cold, but not enough to do me any good. Then I shoved off and unlocked the door, knowing that nothing I could do for myself would give me enough relief to be worth the hassle.

As the door slid open, a black-clad arm came through, then a shoulder, and suddenly Terry and Yasmin were in there with me and the door was shut and locked again.

"Sudden attack of patriotism," Terry announced with a lupine grin. "Have to prevent that international incident. It's a tough job, but somebody's gotta do it."

"You and who else?"

"Just me. Our little princess is going to keep real quiet, now and forever, in return for letting her watch. No accusations, false or otherwise."

I looked at Yasmin. Her eyes were avid. "I swear on my mother's grave," she said, and then, as I still looked skeptical, added, "on my sister's grave!" Somehow, that was convincing. Just the same, I unhooked the cuffs from my belt and snapped them around her wrists with paper towels for padding, then pinned her to the door handle. When I turned back to Terry, the quirk of her brow told me I'd tacitly agreed.

To what, I wasn't sure. We sized each other up for a minute like wrestlers considering grips. Then Terry made her move, trying to press me against the wall with her body, and I reflexively raised a knee to fend her off. Her cock against my kneecap made me feel naked. I'm used to being the hard body in these encounters. I know the steps to this dance, but I've never had to do them backward.

She retreated a few inches. "Gonna stay in uniform?" she asked, eyeing my badge. I unpinned it, slipped it into my holster, unfastened my belt, and hung the whole deal on a coat hook.

"Civilian enough for you?"

"Hell, no! The least you could do is show me your tits."

I stared her in the eyes for a second—somehow I'd never noticed how green they could get—and started to unbutton my shirt. I wasn't sure yet just where I might draw the line. I hung my shirt and sports bra over the gun and holster, even yanked my hair loose from its knot and let it flow over my shoulders. It would have come down anyway.

"So how about you?" She had left her jacket behind but wore a tight-cut leather vest over a black silk shirt.

She was observing me with such interest that she might not have heard. "Breasts like pomegranates," she said softly. "Round and high and tight. Jeez, don't they have gravity in New Hampshire?"

I looked down at myself. My nipples were hardening under an independent impulse. I grabbed Terry's vest and pulled her close to mash the studded leather hard against me, then eased up to rub languorously against it. The leather felt intriguing enough that I didn't push the issue of her staying dressed. And Katzi had accused me of never trying anything different!

Terry pressed closer. I leaned my mouth against her ear. "Pomegranates? Christ, Terry, is that the kind of tripe you write?"

"Yeah, sometimes, when the inspiration's right. But I usually edit it out later." She eased back and looked me over. "I don't suppose," she said, somewhat wistfully, "you could jiggle a little for me?"

"In your dreams!" We were both a bit short of breath now, both struggling with the question of who'd get to do what to whom. Much as my flesh wanted to be touched, my instinct was to lash out if she tried.

"In my dreams?" There was such an odd look in her eyes that I didn't notice that she'd raised her hands until they almost brushed the outer curve of my breasts. "In my dreams," she murmured, just barely stroking me, "you're wearing red velvet."

I hadn't thought of that dress in years. Maybe the last one I ever wore. She'd worn black satin. A college mixer, some clumsy groping in a broom closet, a few weeks of feverish euphoria—then the realization that instead of striking sparks we were more apt to knock chips off each other. Eventually, in fact, we had. I ran my tongue over my reconstructed teeth.

Terry telegraphed an attempt at a kiss, but I wasn't quite ready for that. I let her cup my breasts and rub her thumbs over my appreciative nipples. "One-time only offer," I said, "for old times' sake," and pulled her head downward. She nuzzled the hollow of my throat while I ran my fingers through her crisp brush-cut. Then she went lower, her open mouth wet and hot on my skin, and by the time she was biting where it really mattered her knee was working between my thighs and I was rubbing against it like a cat in heat.

"Come on," I muttered, "show me what you've got!" I groped the bulge in her crotch, and then, while she unbuckled and unbuttoned and rearranged her gear for action, I kicked off my boots and pants.

She tried to clinch too fast. I let her grab my ass for a few seconds, then grabbed hers and shoved her leather pants back far enough that I could get a good look at what had been pressing between my legs.

"State of the art, huh?" Ten thick inches of glistening black high-tech cock, slippery even when not wet. At another time I'd have been envious. Hell, I *was* envious.

"This one's mostly for show," she muttered. "Are you sure...." But it was too late not to be sure.

"I can handle it," I said. And I did handle it, working it with my hand, making her pant and squirm. I manipulated it so that the tip just licked at me, then leaned into it, and for long seconds we were linked in co-ownership of the black cock, clits zinged by a current keen as electricity but far sweeter. Then the slick material skidded in my natural lube and slid along my wet folds, and I spread for it and took it in just an inch or two.

*Can't hurt to see how the other half lives*, I thought, and then, as Terry pressed harder, I remembered the size of what I was dealing with and realized that yeah, it might hurt, and yeah, I might just like it that way.

She pulled back a little and thrust again, and I opened up more, and she plunged harder, building into a compelling rhythm. I gripped the safety railing behind me and tilted my hips to take her deeper inside, aching for even more pounding.

But I had to go after it myself. "Let me move!" I growled.

Terry, uncomprehending, resisted my efforts to swing her around. The black cock, glistening for real now, slipped out as we grappled together.

We were pretty evenly matched in strength. She was a bit beefier; I was taller. She'd been working out with weights and machines; I'd been working over smart-ass punks and pot-bellied drunks. The tie-breaker was that I needed it more.

"You get to wear it; just shut up and let me work it!" I had her back against the railing now. I grabbed the slippery cock and held it steady just long enough to get it where I needed it. Then I swung into serious action.

She flashed a grin and muttered "Fair enough!" Then it was all she could do to hang onto the railing and meet my lunges. The train swayed and rattled, but I rode it, my legs automatically absorbing the shifts, as I rode her black cock, train to my tunnel, bound for glory. The surging hunger got me so slippery that, in spite of its bulk and hardness, what filled me might not have been enough, except that my clit seemed to swell inward as well as outward, and my whole cunt clenched fiercely around the maddening pressure.

Yasmin was emitting little squeals and whimpers; I glanced at her just long enough to notice that one hand, pulled free of the too-hastily fastened cuffs, was busy between her legs.

Terry's grunts turned into moans; she grabbed my hips and dug her fingers into my naked flesh. "Steady...damn it... steady..." she said between clenched teeth, and before I knew what was happening, she forced me back against the hard edge of the sink.

"Hang on," I said, and swung us both around, not losing an inch this time, until my back was to the wall. I couldn't stop moving but managed to slow enough to match her rhythm and grab her leather-covered ass. Her muscles bunched as her hips bucked. I mashed my mouth into hers to catch the eruption of harsh groans, but she had to breathe, and anyway, it didn't matter how much noise she made. I felt my eruption coming and knew there was no way in hell I could muffle it. And didn't give a damn.

I held on until Terry's breathing subsided from wrenching to merely hard. She didn't resist as I turned her again and accelerated into my own demanding beat. I saw her face through a haze, and there may have been pain on it, but she didn't flinch, just kept her hips tilted at the optimum angle for me to ram myself down onto what she offered. My clit clenched like a fist, harder and harder each time I drove toward her. A sound like a distant train whistle seemed to come closer and closer, the reverberations penetrating into places deeper than I had even known existed.

Then it hit. My clit went off like a brass gong, and waves smashed up against the explosion raging outward from my center. A storm of sound engulfed me.

Terry held me for the hours it seemed to take for me to suck in enough breath to see straight. Finally I slouched back against the edge of the sink, letting the slippery cock emerge inch by inch. She reached past me to grab a handful of paper towels; I took them away from her and slowly wiped my juices from the glistening black surface. When I aimed the used towels toward the trash container, she stopped me, folded them inside a clean one, and tucked them into her pocket, avoiding my eyes. I didn't ask.

Then she looked toward the door. As I'd been vaguely aware, Yasmin had been rubbing herself into a frenzy, apparently with some success. "So, Princess," Terry said with the old jaunty quirk of her brow, "didn't I tell you it'd be worth it just to listen to her come? I could tape that song and make a bundle."

"You, Terry, are a prick," I said lazily, "and I mean that, of course, in the best possible sense of the word."

"I still get the shivers now and then," Terry went on, nominally speaking to Yasmin, "thinking of that alto sax wailing. The final trumpet fanfare this time, though, was better than anything I remember."

"Jeez, I hope you edit out that kind of crap!" I said, and turned to the sink to clean up. The mirror was so steamed I couldn't see a thing. Then I dressed, feeling more secure with my gun belt around my hips. Not that security is everything.

The rest of the trip wasn't bad. The whispers and surreptitious looks from the college kids and a few others who must have heard us were kind of a kick. Yasmin watched sleepily as Terry and I chatted about old times, old acquaintances, and the intervening years. Terry got off at Penn Station, offering me a book at the last minute with her card tucked into it. I took out the card and slipped it into my breast pocket, behind the badge.

"Moving a little stiffly, aren't we?" I said as I helped get her duffel down from the rack.

"Mmm, but the show must go on."

"I'm sure you won't disappoint your audience." I aimed an encouraging slap at her fine, muscular ass. "Go get 'em."

Yasmin made a few tentative advances between New York and D.C., but I wasn't that vulnerable anymore, and she gave up and slept for most of the trip. The welcoming party at Union Station was headed by a tall, mature woman in a well-cut dark suit.

"The Princess traveled well?" she asked, with a keen, hard look at me.

"Just fine," I said, meeting her eyes frankly, "with no harm done, if you don't count a few slaps to make her keep her hands to herself."

"Excellent," she said, with the ghost of a smile. "The Sultan would be happy to offer hospitality for the night, before your return trip."

"I appreciate the offer," I said truthfully, "but I have other plans. I'm getting on the next train to New York. There's a literary event I don't want to miss."

Terry's schedule of readings was scrawled on the back of her card. There's a special one at midnight. I have a notion there'll be enough erotica groupies to go around. Beyond that, I wouldn't mind meeting an editor, finding out more about the writing game. I know damned well that Terry will want to use some of today's action in her fiction. I might just beat her to it.

I've gotta edit out that "train to my tunnel, bound for glory" line, though. Too bad. That's sure as hell exactly how it felt.

# Twisted Beauty

*Elspeth Potter*

One Tuesday, Alex took Sylvia to Hong's Special Famous in San Francisco, his favorite restaurant because of its commodious and solid wheelchair ramp. He liked being able to enter a place beside his date, briskly propelling himself, instead of bumping clumsily over doorsills and fending off metal handles that tried to smack him in the face. He had always hated appearing a buffoon; and since the accident that had crushed his legs, he needed all the confidence he could get.

Having a beautiful woman beside him, if no longer on his arm, helped considerably. Constanza, his first girlfriend after he'd returned to his life, was a busty blonde paralegal from the contracts department of his firm. She always wore snug power suits that showed most of her shiny nylons; not his type, ordinarily, but entering a room with her sent a clear message to other men, a message in which Alex took savage delight: *Yes, cripples have sex, and they're having hotter sex than you*. Except he hadn't been. With Constanza, he'd been too nervous in private to get it up, much less suggest any more exotic activities.

Good-hearted Mary had been next; she'd done extensive research on spinal injuries on the Web, and arrived at his apartment prepared to help him with all sorts of private bodily functions that he could manage perfectly well on his own. His spine wasn't damaged: Only his legs had been splintered like sugar cane, scarred and bent out of all recognition. He and Mary had managed a little fucking, because by then he'd been in dire straits and not about to turn down sex if it was offered. But being Mary's charity case, however much she denied it, quickly palled, and he'd been relieved when she'd left him for Topher the water skiing instructor.

Sylvia was different.

Sylvia was comfortable enough with him that she made fun, as he had learned to, of his struggle with everyday tasks like reaching the top buttons in an elevator. Her teasing put him at ease, as if his twisted legs were merely a delightful, kinky sex toy. She kept him so involved in sensation that he had no opportunity to obsess about his appearance, his awkwardness in certain positions, or the uncontrollable spasms of pain and cramping that sometimes interrupted them in the heat of the moment. He could hardly comprehend the sheer relief of regular sex without pity.

Even considered objectively, their sex had been fantastic, as good as any he remembered from before, perhaps better. Sylvia demanded, and he rose to her challenge.

Tonight's trip to Hong's was part of a pattern they were establishing together. They ordered, and Alex deftly stripped the paper from his chopsticks, snapped them apart, and used them to place deep-fried noodles dipped in duck sauce between Sylvia's full lips. Then, between one breath and the next, he found himself fixated on her neatly manicured fingers enfolding the round, handle-less teacup, his gut fluttering as she expounded on new albums they'd received at the radio station that week, and related anecdotes of her promotional trip to a music festival, minutiae that suddenly loomed larger to him than global warming. They'd been lovers for two months, but only now did he know he was in love with her. And Sylvia with him? How would he know?

What if she wasn't? If she didn't love him, would she leave him, like the others had? If she didn't love him, would he want her to stay?

After dinner, Sylvia drove them to her house in Suttontown, Alex talking about the ocean dumping case that had landed on his desk that day, a case he thought he had a chance of winning. She seemed interested in what he had to say, but no more than usual. Did she sense the new intensity he felt? In the twilight they swam in the pool, laughing and slipping in and out of each other's grip like sea lions playing. He was no longer able to free climb, but he felt almost as free in the water. Later, in Sylvia's living room, he sat naked on her enormous Turkish rug, wishing he could feel its softness on the backs of his thighs. A single lamp pooled bronze light on the rug's jewel tones, showing her pale skin, his darker skin, and Sylvia's damp auburn curls. She knelt in front of him and began to dry his hair with short, luxurious strokes, complaining of how thick it was. "No Rogaine in your future, Sasha," she said.

Alex needed to touch her. He needed all of her, but he sat still, waiting, knowing she liked to lead their encounters.

Sylvia tenderly combed her fingers through his hair. His scalp prickled, and warmth cascaded down his spine. She trapped him with her gray gaze, her eyes seeming to say, *You are mine.* She rubbed his ears gently between her fingers, just on the edge of roughness: first the tops, then the lobes, then up the outer rim, then her cool fingers slipped inside his ear canal, and out again, and up to the tops, and down, and....

"You're drowning me," he said dizzily.

"You don't want me to stop."

"No," he said. "Yes." The heat in his belly wasn't enough. He couldn't sense what she felt. He had to touch her or die. He swayed forward. She pulled back.

"Tell me what you want," Sylvia said, so close to his mouth he could feel her rapid breaths. "I want to hear you say it. Then I'll let you touch me."

"Kiss me," he said. "Now."

They toppled and rolled, her body pressing softly to the length of his, her warmth almost agony. Each heartbeat thrust him more tightly against her. He stroked her with hot hands and flushed face, and sucked her tongue into his mouth, hearing throaty sounds of pleasure. His.

She pulled away and grinned; her hand cupped his scrotum and his muscles clenched. He wouldn't come. He wouldn't. He hadn't figured this out yet, how she felt. His unbearable tension faded over the next few seconds, and he loosened his fingers from her waist, one at a time. The velvet of her cheek stroked near his mouth; one hand smoothed absentmindedly over his ribs; her free hand caressed his balls, feather-like, each touch distinct.

Sylvia murmured, "Let me—let me do it all." She trailed her silky-smooth knuckles along his cock, an easier sensation to tolerate than her evanescent brushes against his balls, until she swirled a finger under the edge of his foreskin, rubbing it gently between finger and thumb, sliding the skin forward and back, ignoring the dripping head. A soft groan escaped his teeth and he reached for her; Sylvia pushed his hands away, pressing them to the carpet. He contracted his belly so hard that it hurt.

Sylvia squeezed his balls lightly and Alex sucked in a breath. "You look intense," she said. "I love it that I can do this to you." She disentangled from him and sat up, not letting go, her thumb and forefinger teasing his cock deliberately, with more pressure now. His entire life spiraled down to those two fingers. "Like this...you're beautiful."

Did she really think that? His twisted legs bore no resemblance to her flawless curves. If only she knew how radiant she looked when he buried himself deep within her body. That was love, wasn't it, when the other person was the most beautiful you'd ever seen? Sylvia, nude, was that person. He trembled at the mere thought of it. He arched his neck as his muscles spasmed, but he didn't ask her to stop and wait for him. He was afraid to try to speak in this half-world between desire and culmination.

"Close your eyes," Sylvia said.

Compelled to obey, Alex closed them. Sylvia released his cock and he relaxed fractionally, as her soft hands passed over his hair, his face, down his chest. "How do you want to finish this?" she whispered into his ear.

It seemed years since he'd made a decision. He opened his eyes to see Sylvia's face above him. "Us," he said. "Together."

Sylvia bent closer. "Me on top?"

He was too far gone to laugh. "My turn."

"Beg me," she said.

He didn't want to play this time, but he would do anything. "Sylvia, please."

Sylvia stretched out with him, and he sighed and shivered as her skin contacted his. "If I don't, right now...." With this disjointed sentence nagging at him, he twisted atop and slickly into her in one motion, attempting to merge with her whole being, not just her body. He tried to catch his breath, but her inner muscles contracted and in one ignominious instant it was too late for control.

No matter what people said, coming was nothing like falling.

A few minutes later, still shaking with reaction, he laughed a little and said, "You did that on purpose."

Sylvia rolled sideways, bringing him with her, and stroked up and down his back. His muscles fell limp under her hands, even as his throat tightened with exhaustion or emotion, he couldn't tell which. He'd wanted it to last longer. He cupped her ass and pressed her against him to savor the erratic pulse of her cunt as their bodies relaxed. The rug exuded their musk, like incense.

"Tell me you liked it," she said. Her leg hooked around his; he felt it at his hip.

Alex met her eyes, a foggy gray universe in the blur of her face. "Yes," he said. He kissed her, slowly, the barest touch of his tongue to the damp gloss inside her lower lip. Truthfully, he was relieved his stamina hadn't been tested, after having been on the verge of explosion ever since that moment at Hong's.

"Ex-cellent," she purred in a fake villain accent, trailing a finger down his chest, lighthearted as always, a surface Alex longed to penetrate. Tonight, he'd bitten away only her pale lipstick.

"And you?" he asked.

"None of your business," she said, grinning.

Alex pulled her against him, suddenly exalted like dawn in the Grand Tetons, rapturous from love and from fear. Sylvia curled against him and they lay, quietly, while outside, rain spattered against the patio.

# Reconstructing Richard

*Helen Settimana*

The last time I saw Richard he was striding across the tarmac of the runway with a duffel bag on his back, heavy olive green trousers tucked into his boots. His jacket with the small red-and-white embroidered flag on the shoulder was shiny and wet; his special blue beret tipped downward to shield his face from the rain. He didn't turn and wave as he mounted the last step into the plane. He just disappeared. From under an umbrella I watched from the chain-link fence until the plane vanished into low clouds, snarling like an enraged beast.

He wrote every week, letters that recounted the hardship and suffering he observed, the daily peril he endured. They were also letters laden with passion and want. Sarajevo was, he said, hell on earth, a place where incomprehensible savagery played itself out on a daily basis, by the hour, the minute, the second. The once majestic, cultured city had been vivisected by opposing factions. Neighbors killed neighbors, former friends turned upon friends, and it seemed that everyone was harrying the peacekeepers. It wasn't his first tour with the RCR "Third": He believed in the mission, but he confessed to being afraid. How could he not be, in the face of such abomination? How could one fathom Europe's renewed descent into madness? *Europe*. He wanted to be home, but was duty-bound to stay.

*"Carol, I lie in my bunk and think of you and miss you so much it hurts. I can see you in my mind, and that makes it better, but it is still not you, not you really lying with me, substantial and safe. I miss your touch and I miss your smell. I miss the way heat rises off your body when we make love, and the way it keeps coming off you while you sleep, like an internal fire I can't put out. I want to taste you, bathe in your wetness. It would make me feel alive in this dead place. There are bodies rotting in the streets because no one will risk coming to collect them. The snipers are everywhere. I want a moment of you here with me. Send me more pictures, honey, please?"*

I sent him chaste photos taken at the photo booth in the mall, but he asked for more—photos that would help him remember visceral things: the cathartic fucking when he came home on leave with his drab fatigues still on and his boots still laced, kissing me so that I felt that my mouth was fucked, that he had somehow entered my body before his cock was even pressing its way into me. I'd fight him a bit, because he loved the combative edge. He'd come that way, in a few short strokes, and then spend the rest of the night making it up to me. God, he was wonderful.

I set my camera on a tripod and stripped. I stripped for Rich, a couple of thousand miles away in hostile foreign territory where everyone seemed to be an enemy. *Pow!* the flash of the strobe. *Pow!* I shot my tits, and my ass, and a close-up of my pussy, inflamed with the recollection of his touch. I wanted him to see my clit and the juice that made it shine. I threw decorum out the window. I used a candle and a cucumber and the handle of the bayonet from the old Lee-Enfield rifle that had belonged to his grandfather. I vamped. I wrapped my face in a T-shirt of his that I'd rescued from the laundry hamper before he left. I came buckets. *Pow! Pow! Pow!* I gave the film to Cathy, a friend and neighbor who had a darkroom. I blushingly explained what the pictures were for. "No problem," she said, grinning conspiratorially. The photos were ready in a day, and I carefully packaged them with his name and outfit written on the label, and dropped them into the mail bag.

It was about two weeks before his tour was to have ended: I was shoveling the snow that had fallen during the night and cloaked the base in white; the sky was a crisp blue dotted with puffy clouds. A dark car carrying two passengers pulled up the drive in front of our house, and I paused in mid-push, then sank slowly to the pavement. I knew why they were here even before I recognized Major Duncan MacPherson, the base's chaplain. His assistant followed him.

I couldn't hear their carefully rehearsed official words of condolence: Master Corporal Richard Harper, my husband, was dead. The sound was too far off. My ears were filled with the roar of an avalanche. The men moved with a strange, deliberate slowness that made them hard to see, as if all reality were caught in a sticky, viscous gum. My tongue stuck to the roof of my mouth. Tiny sprinkles of brilliant snow fell around me; incongruously, I was aware they were melting on my glasses.

*Richard was dead.* Distantly I heard a woman's voice saying, "No, no, no.... This is a joke, right? Tell me it's a joke...come on...*come on.*"

"Mrs. Harper? Carol?" Their words still came with the force and finality of an evisceration. I hardly remember them. I was rocking on the freezing sidewalk, feeling for all the world as if my guts were spilling out. I tried to stuff it all back in: each loop, my love, our passion, our future. I tried to hold to the vision of a better house, car, a real life in a real neighborhood after all of this; *all of this* running through my mind, my fingers; resisting my attempts to return it home and sew it up safely inside. Someone took my arm and we floated like phantoms toward the house. They guided me inside. I remember offering coffee, which was declined. My hands were shaking too much to be of use, anyway.

"How?"

"Richard was accompanying a convoy, transporting displaced children from a camp to a makeshift orphanage in a school outside Sarajevo. The convoy had clear UN markings. He was riding in the back of the truck. They had been guaranteed safe passage. The vehicles stopped for a moment at a crossroad, and he climbed out of the back to, ah, relieve himself. He was hit in the head by sniper fire. When he fell forward he triggered a landmine." I didn't hear the rest.

"Would you like someone to stay with you?'

"Huh?"

"Would you like someone to stay with you? I think you should. Is there anyone we can call to come here?"

"Um, no…I mean yes, yes…I should do something…I should call my parents…. Oh my God, his parents need to be told!"

"That's been taken care of, Carol. We'll look after everything else, too." The assistant was already on the phone.

It was on the six o'clock news. Richard and three children dead. A dozen others wounded.

He was home in a week—the small box that contained all of him that could be salvaged, that is. His friend Trevor, who had been injured in the back of the truck, came too, hobbling on crutches. At the gravesite MacPherson said some words, with his black robes fluttering in the cold wind. He wore black leather gloves. Gunners fired three times into the air as the honor guard stood at attention. A piper played a *lament*. People said consoling things and helped me with the wake, but home was soon enough empty: a lousy, fucking government-issue two-story row house, uglier than some of the projects in the worst parts of town. Still, it was our home. I was used to his absence, but this time there would be no end to the emptiness. I gave his clothes to Goodwill. I made a list and packed boxes with old photos and stacked them with the rest of our family memorabilia. I moved to an apartment. When the snow thawed I planted poppies in my window box and waited for them to grow.

This is the thing that links me to the women of my past. They were all army wives—three generations, at least. Some years before, I'd helped my mother clear boxes stored in her home. We found letters from my great-grandfather to his wife, penned in France during the Great War. Large blocks of text had been stricken out by the censors, but others were love letters, untouched, penciled in his sloping, slightly florid hand. I strained to read them. They sounded like Richard's notes, but couched in the reserved manner of the day. "My dearest Etta, my thoughts are with you every day and I yearn for the time we may be re-united." *"May be."* The uncertainty of war. I looked for hidden meanings in the letters, an arcane code of passion, but they were full of sweet *tristesse* and noble longing. They had been married three days before he was shipped to France. I saw their wedding photo. She looked like a pagan pre-Raphaelite bride, with a daisy chain headpiece and trailing ribbons. He looked like T. E. Lawrence in his dress uniform and officer's walking stick. Handsome as hell.

I opened an envelope yellowed with age, and there it was: news of my great-grandfather's death in the muddy, stinking trenches filled with the dead and blood, piss and shit and all manner of horror. I wonder if Etta, pregnant with their only child, fainted when the courier brought it to her door. He'd have ridden up her walkway on a black bike with fat tires and an oversized horn; a raven-like harbinger of death fluttering up to a house bravely bedecked in Victory bunting. Did he doff his cap to her? Did he look for a tip?

I think I went mad.

Richard came to me in dreams, looking like a crow in a black beret with a priapic cock bobbing obscenely before him. I lay down, spread myself for him, gazed at him coquettishly— glad to see him up to his old form. I was desperate, with the kind of desire that haunts the dreams of the impaired and insane. When he entered me I felt a searing pain shoot through my face, but I came with an intensity so great that I woke up panting and found my sheets wet.

If I was lucky I would fall into sleep and he would be there, waiting for me, his hair shorn, small ears tight against his head, hard and smiling. We would wrestle frantically, and when he entered me I would dissolve into a million motes of light and drift toward oblivion. On a good night I could come in my sleep, but in waking, all passion eluded me.

On a bad night I was digging in his grave, mad with desire and grief and the need to find him. I dug my way to Sarajevo, emerging like a mole into the debris of a raped urban land-scape. I would wake up screaming.

Sometimes he came in the guise of a young boy with a huge rifle on his shoulder. He'd march out of the fog blanketing the blasted city—hollow-eyed, but with Richard's young face. He'd aim the gun at me and then, laughing, turn it upon itself. *Bang*. The swirling fog turned pink. No head.

"Cath, I have to go to Bosnia," I said.

"Good God, Carol, whatever for?"

I started to cry—long, sniffling, hiccuping sobs. Cathy looked absently out of my kitchen window: She was not comfortable with my pain.

"I think I'm going nuts. I have to see the place. I feel like if I could just *see* the place I could let him go or something. *I see him on street corners.* I *saw* him at the Monument and I keep having these dreams that seem to tell me to go. *I have to go.* Things are more settled there now. People are making their way back. I just want to see where it happened, and try to understand. God, Cathy, I just have to try to understand what happened to him."

Two months later I found myself in the back of a battered car with Trevor beside me. From Zagreb, Croatia, we had been driven into the Bosnian heartland. We lurched through untended potholes in the streets of the capital. An hour later, on a low rise in the crotch of a valley flanked by steep rocky hills, we came to a crossroad. The car stopped. The roadsides had been swept for mines. There was not a tree in sight, just rocks, burnt stumps and scrub grass, low bushes and shell craters. A disturbing, sweetish smell hung in the air. Skeletons of burnt buildings, vehicles, and farm equipment lay in the fields. A wide hole filled with water pocked the grassy verge of the roadside. Trevor motioned to it, and looked away. To my surprise I found some plastic flowers lying at the rim of the hole. I looked for bloodstains in the gravel, some further evidence of his life passing here. I picked up something that looked like a stone. It was a shard of pottery marked with incisions, the indestructible evidence of past life, civilization. It was very old.

"This is it?" I asked, incredulous. I stared at the flowers near the crater. "Where was the sniper?"

"We don't really know, but we think the shot came from over there," he said, pointing at what appeared to be a blank hillside.

*"There?"*

"Carol, the hills are occupied by people who have lived here for hundreds, thousands of years—if they don't want to be seen, they won't be."

I took out my camera and recorded everything: the ruins in the field, the scummy water in the crater, the potsherd, the cheap flowers, and Trevor's suddenly old face reflected in the car's window. Then I sat on the road and cried as if I would never stop. The driver smoked a cigarette and wandered down the road until he disappeared from sight. Trevor eased himself beside me, sat in the summer grass with his arm around my shoulder, and let me collapse, heaving, into him. There was no sense to what had happened. None at all. They had come here to do good and in the middle of this blasted place Richard lost his life. I felt dehydrated by the time we turned around and headed back. I could see myself in the glass of the sedan; I looked like hell. I leaned into Trevor and quaked. He kissed my forehead and my cheek, and in a fit of madness I took his face in my hands and kissed his mouth like I meant to eat it: lips first, then teeth, then tongue. His eyes were bright and wet.

He was quiet and respectful, almost reverential. He undressed with his back to me and said to the wall, "I'm not Richard, Carol, I'm not...."

I pressed myself into his back, feeling the warmth of him against my breasts, the front of my thighs. I knew that, and I didn't care. He was another link to Richard, and to something else I would never understand. My hands traced the center line of his belly, and tangled in the tight nap of hair in his groin, down to the heated thickness of him bobbing in mid-air. He was hard, his cock weeping, but he moved carefully, deliberately. I closed my eyes and tried to recall Rich, to feel his hands and his mouth and his cock on and in me, but Trevor was slower, and gentler, and he smelled different, too. The jagged gash left by the shrapnel from the mine stood out, livid purple, puckered into his thigh. I ran my fingers along it, traced its erratic course: the map of our joint disaster. He kissed my burning eyelids, and my mouth, tender from gnawing at my own lips. He muttered something about not being able to account for his recent whereabouts, and I heard the snap of latex being unrolled. I yearned to be taken, devoured, and possessed, so I thrashed and clawed and called, as if by encouraging him to greater passion I could reconstruct Richard and his savage love. Finally, Trevor held me down and opened me up and filled me until I hurt, until I came, until I cried again. We did this over and over until I was wrung of all moisture, and then we slept together, his cock still clasped inside me, dangerously. I didn't care and Rich could not have minded.

In the morning, Trevor seemed embarrassed. He lay back and put his hands over his face and kept saying that he felt guilty about "taking advantage" of me, but I kissed him on the mouth and held his head and told him not to worry, I was going to be just fine, just fine indeed. It was only a matter of time.

Back home, I began to write. I wrote what I missed about Rich—the strength of him, his commitment. I wrote about the war: how a conflict so far away and so unconnected to us could reach out and hammer away at my safety. Mostly I wrote about sex, the cement that held us together; the way he had made me feel, the sensations, the emotions, the colors, and the scents—the essence of him. I came to believe that to write is to make the mortal immortal; to create anything is to be in a small way in harmony with the divine: alive. If I could give form to what I had lost, I could make it whole and let it go. In reconstructing Richard I could say goodbye at last.

Over time, the dreams and nightmares receded. I was able to take Rich's picture out of the box and put it up on the bookcase in my studio again, along with the pictures of my great-grandfather. Richard is in me always: He is the engine that stokes my creation and my desire. But now in the center of the mantle stands a large shot of Trevor and me in front of our trailer in Algonquin Park, hemmed in by towering red pines. The smoke of our campfire fogs the air behind us. Alive, I wanted to see the trees—the tall, fragrant trees.

# Schoolgirl's Delight

*Talia Brahm*

Finally alone. She had endured the crowds of well-wishers and their simpering condolences. She'd survived the mindless chatter throughout the wake, and then the funeral. Now she was finally, blessedly alone.

Had her parents had that many friends? No, friends imply pleasant times. And her parents would endure no such evil. They had seen this world as a test. Pleasure was evil, a temptation to be resisted. By contrast, Becky saw the world as a brimming cornucopia of gifts to be savored. Watermelon juice ran down your chin for a reason. It was meant to be sweet and sticky, a cool delight on a sweltering day.

But her grim parents had been habitual churchgoers, and every church member came to show their grief. Or maybe they just came to see the show – her show: "The Prodigal Daughter Returns."

The church ladies dabbed appropriately at their eyes, even as they icily appraised her short skirt. What were they so upset about? Her entire outfit was funeral black, from her low-cut top to her stiletto heels—well, except for the furiously pink scarf that flirted with her cleavage. Even her thong panties were appropriately somber black. Becky sighed. Let the biddies stare.

The men stared too, when their wives weren't looking. Especially Zack. Zack had been the fantasy of her high school years: Zack Jones, captain of the football team, the hand-somest boy in three counties. And he was Marsha Moore's steady. Was there some unwritten rule that the football captain had to date the head cheerleader?

Becky had left this narrow-minded little town right after high school, but her mother felt compelled to keep her up to date with her former classmates—as if any of them cared what she was doing. Zack and Marsha had married right after college, then moved back here. Zack opened the only insurance office/real estate brokerage in town. Marsha was lousy with diamonds and Zack sported several ostentatious gold rings himself. They were the perfect couple—perfectly miserable, from what Becky could see.

After the service, the men offered Becky consoling hugs: tight, grasping hugs. Zack was itching for his turn, watching for an opportunity. He found it when Marsha excused herself to the ladies' room. She was gone a long time— gossiping with her friends about Becky, no doubt. Some things never change—except that Zack was holding her now. She drank in his sweet, male scent as he clung to the sensuous warmth he would not find at home. When Marsha returned, she didn't like that scene one little bit.

Becky had returned to her parents' home, alone.

The refrigerator was nearly bare, as it had always been. Becky remembered going home with her best friend Jenna after school one day and being greeted by the enticing aroma of fresh-baked cookies. Becky had stuffed her mouth with warm crunch and hot, melting chocolate. All that ever greeted her at home was the steady hum of Mommy's sewing machine and an empty, echoing fridge.

But Becky had learned to take care of herself, and she had brought her own supplies. She slaked her thirst with an icy bottle of spring water and grabbed a bar of dark chocolate. Her parents would never have indulged themselves this way. Becky never denied herself. She indulged, never accepting anything less than the best. She was as a result profoundly satisfied. Someday, she told herself, she might test the same theory with men. Someday.

Becky wandered into her old bedroom. Her parents hadn't changed a thing. Her high school uniform was still hanging on the closet door. She had neatly hung it there after the last day of school, swearing she would never again be seen in anything so unattractive. Private schools seem to have an uncanny knack for finding the ugliest materials and fashioning them into even uglier designs. Below the skirt, her black-and-white saddle shoes stood waiting, as if they expected her speedy return. In truth it had been five years and she had worn nothing but high heels ever since.

Removing the hanger from its hook, she uncovered a full-length mirror. That had been a hard-fought battle. She had won Daddy over by insisting she wasn't vain, vanity being one of the seven deadly sins. No, her intentions were pure: She needed this mirror to wage war against the deadly sin of lust. How else could she be certain that she was dressed modestly? How else to reassure herself that her burgeoning body was properly camouflaged, lest it incite lustful desires in the hearts of her male classmates?

She appraised herself now in the mirror. The skirt was a bit too short, the low-cut top a bit too snug. The scarf was definitely too bright. Yes, the woman reflected in the mirror was indeed vain, and she loved inciting lustful thoughts in the hearts of men.

Impulsively, she slipped off her "mourning" outfit, leaving only her high heels, black push-up bra, and matching thong panties. She slipped on the red plaid skirt and shed her panties—the two simply didn't work together. She took the white oxford collar shirt from the hanger and put it on. The black lace of her bra threatened to erupt from behind the starched white buttons, so she deftly removed it and modestly buttoned the shirt all the way up. Her pampered nipples were shocked by the rough cotton. They stood erect as if questioning why their silken haven had disappeared.

The heels must go too, she told herself. Changing into ankle socks and saddle shoes was a shock to her feet, but now the look was complete. This was what her parents had wanted—except for those demanding nipples pressing pink against the shirt, protesting such barbaric treatment.

Frowning, Becky remembered her high-school protests. The skirt was so long, so ugly. She'd begged Mommy to hem it up short, like the popular girls did. Mommy hesitated but relented. Becky remembered the sewing machine's hum from across the hall as she'd stood before this very mirror, fantasizing.

Throngs of boys surrounded her in her short little skirt, all vying for her attention. Even Jan Jenkins wouldn't have more boyfriends than she. Maybe she'd take pity on the other girls, the way they never did to her, and share some of those boys. She'd share with Jenna, anyway. "If you go out with my friend Jenna, I'll let you kiss me," she'd tell the boys. And then there was Zack. She'd definitely steal Zack from Marsha.

Her delicious fantasy had been interrupted by Mommy's return. Eagerly she'd put the redeemed skirt on, only to burst into tears. Mommy had taken only an inch, maybe half an inch, off the bottom. It wasn't worth the electricity it took to run the sewing machine.

"Best I could do. What would Daddy say?" Becky remembered it all. She'd known then, there would be no Zack in her life, no throngs of high-school admirers.

"Well, I'm not fourteen anymore," she declared now. Dashing to the sewing room, she grabbed the scissors and raced back to the mirror. Shedding the skirt, she bent over the bed, forming a lovely mirror image of her naked rear framed by the virginal white shirt and the clunky, good-girl shoes. She peeked over her shoulder: Oh my, she thought, what a naughty girl.

Her work done, she slid back into the skirt—a much shorter skirt. Somehow it didn't seem so ugly now that there was the possibility of a glimpse of pussy fur— if she'd had much pussy fur. She'd begun shaving to look presentable in a bikini, then in a skimpier bikini. Then Joel had come into her life. Joel had an acrobatic tongue and a penchant for oral sex—and he liked naked pussy. She'd started shaving her lips for him—and discovered she liked the look and feel of it.

She wondered if Zack liked naked pussy. Flashing the mirror, she taunted him. "Look what you missed out on, Zack." Turning her back, she wiggled her butt, the shortened skirt revealing tantalizing glimpses of firm, white flesh. She loved her body, despite her upbringing. Her therapist had been horrified at her parents' stifling inhibitions and the resulting damage to Becky's self-image. But even as a child, Becky had realized that it wasn't merely the body, it was life in general that her parents feared. Becky wouldn't make the same mistake.

That's why she'd gotten into therapy—that, and her last lover, Thomas. Thomas was sweet, but he was a little uptight, and he was intimidated by her appetites. It hurt to lose him, but she wanted to experience all the pleasures of life. Now, she felt that something was missing. Her therapist assured her it was never a man, but a part of herself that she was missing.

Still...Thomas would love this outfit. Sadly, she leaned on the edge of the bed, facing the mirror. Thomas. Her hand found the wet spot between her legs. Leaning back, she could taste his kisses, and began to feel better. She could almost feel his hard cock inside her—or was that her fingers? Laughing, she caught her reflection. Yep, those were her fingers. Sweet little schoolgirl, indeed. "Well, guys, you really blew it," she said to her fantasy admirers.

She shoved her fingers further into her pussy, then cradled them back and forth, in and out, watching herself in the mirror. Double pleasure: watching and touching. Might as well go for a triple, she thought. She lifted her fingers to her lips and gently sucked her own salty sweetness from them. Joel had taught her to appreciate her own taste, as well as his. She returned for more. Her pussy grasped at her fingers, wanting to keep them inside. But she took them back anyway to once again lick her own flavor. Her pussy was eager for her penetrating digits, though, so Becky gave in. Spreading her legs, she watched them thrust and retreat, thrust and retreat. Her clit was swelling now as the ball of her hand brushed over it and she pushed her fingers deeper. Sweet convulsions overcame her. Her juices flowed, and she thought of Zack. "This could've been yours," she told him. "Loser."

She dozed off and woke with sticky fingers and a smile on her lips. Even before she opened her eyes, she had the distinct impression she was being watched. When she finally opened them, Zack was standing beside her bed. Maybe she was dreaming.

"The front door was unlocked." Then he was beside her on the bed. His hands roamed her body, without invitation, and, quite honestly, without much effect; at least, it wasn't doing much for Becky. Zack was breathing hard, roughly rubbing his groin against her leg. How often had she fantasized this very scene: Zack hungry for her, wanting her. In her imagination, she gave him what he wanted, because she wanted it too. But that had been ten years ago.

She slid her fingers into her pussy once again, letting her juices cover them. Then, putting her fingers to Zack's lips, she watched his eyes widen as his tongue savored its first taste of her pussy. He lost control, sucking her fingers so hard that she thought he would swallow them. He fumbled for the zipper on his pants. Becky stopped him.

"You're too late, Zack. Go home to Marsha."

She escorted him to the front door. He made one last attempt—pressing against her as if to impress her with his hard-on. It didn't work.

Becky watched him gun the engine of his shiny black Stealth and angrily squeal the tires as he sped down the street. She closed the door, this time waiting for the reassuring clink of locking tumblers.

She was finally, blessedly alone.

# Stone, Still

*A. R. Morlan*

"They can't force me to do this."

Pieretta let the letter from the government fall from her stiffened fingers. The single sheet of watermarked paper see-sawed in the air as it descended, then landed on the floor at her feet with the free ends of the trifold upright, much like a curled, drying autumn leaf whose stem and tip came close to touching.

Pieretta's caregiver (exactly which one she was, Doreen or Geri or that slow, overweight one whose name Pieretta never did bother to recall, was something Pieretta refused to think about anymore—mentally, she allowed the women to merge into one, intrusive being, flitting just beyond her limited range of vision like sooty dust motes to be endured, nothing more) shook her head and said, "But this should do you good—it's for everyone's good. I read you those studies, from the papers—the government's established that being in a nurturing, sexual relationship is of benefit to all people."

"You've just said the magic word—'People!' Not," she said, looking down at her shiny-skinned, stiff arms, bending her neck with difficulty, then adding with as much emphasis as her pulled-back lips would allow, "stiffs."

The caregiver (Doreen? Pieretta dimly recalled this woman saying that name at some time to her) shook her head again, before soothing, "Now, now, that's like a bla—uh, an African-American calling themselves by the 'n' word. Don't degrade yourself like that. Why don't you reread the letter? It plainly states that they've found you an ideal emotional and sexual partner."

Pieretta wished that she could cross her arms in front of her chest, but the best she could manage was a cagelike balling of her hands into near fists. "Yeah, and during his day job, he pickles real stiffs in a...."

"The letter didn't say anything about his occupation, did it?"

*God, spare me from the literal minded,* Pieretta mentally sighed.

Doreen (or Geri?) bent over at the waist, making her fleshy midriff inner tube show under that tight smock she wore, and picked up the letter from the government. Tilting her head back to better see through her bifocals, she began to read aloud:

*"An ideal potential sexual lifemate has been located for you in this city: Mr. Howard Noach is thirty-four years old, a nonsmoker, and currently single/unattached. He has been found to be compatible with your sexual preferences/predilections, and should prove to be a lasting, stable partner. Your first meeting is scheduled for—"*

"Enough. I remember what the letter said."

Doreen kept reading silently, her lips making the occasional moue.

"It doesn't say anything about what he *does.*"

"It doesn't matter, does it?"

Pieretta mentally willed her rigid legs to move, scissorlike, as she walked away from the caregiver. The sun was hitting its highest point in the sky, and its rays became dust motes, swirling warm fingers that caressed her taut skin through the skylight above. She closed her eyes, and briefly fantasized that fervid pressure was a human finger gently stroking her flesh—until she imagined the expression of revulsion on the face of her phantom lover.

Bad enough that she'd been born in a body whose very DNA was tainted with this disease, this *thing* the doctors called scleroderma (and that those less inclined to be politically correct dubbed "stiff's disease"), but to lose not only her mobility, but her very sexuality in the process. Pieretta supposed the latter loss was a fair trade, given that one of the few medications that helped her to even a small degree was Thalomid, which had once been known as thalidomide. For her, procreative sex was impossible, prohibited by morals and law—which is why she'd initially been bemused by the long questionnaire every adult over the age of eighteen had been required to fill out last year. While the forms were a mere technicality for those already married, engaged, or otherwise promised to another (simply a way to untangle potentially sexually incompatible couples before their relationships disintegrated on their own), for those who remained unattached, unloved, unfulfilled in the most intimate sense, the forms were meant to provide salvation. Otherwise they were doomed to depression, short lives, and physical problems—all traceable to a lack of sexual expression.

That things had come to this state of governmental influence in matters heretofore personal and intimate seemed absurd at first—until people remembered how the government had managed to turn a nation of smokers and casual drinkers into an abstaining, ostensibly healthy body-and-psyche-conscious community. Then, despite all the efforts of the government-sponsored do-gooders, when it was discovered that people remained depressed, unhappy, and even defiantly unhealthy, still more grant-funded do-gooders took yet another look at the nation's mental and physical state of being, and decided that the panacea for almost every remaining ill in society rested squarely below everyone's waistline.

Virtually all doctors concurred: Those who stayed single/celibate were cheating themselves of health, happiness, and longevity (religious celibates not included). Pieretta had found those initial articles about this newfound sexual requirement amusing, in a bitter fashion; no matter how many men she might service, not a one of them would make her skin supple again, or release the pervasive stone-like stiffness in her internal organs and tissues. She remembered joking with one of the caregivers that the naysayers had had it wrong all those years—masturbation didn't make people go blind, it actually cured blindness.

The caregiver didn't understand the joke.

Slowly turning her head, Pieretta said to Doreen, "I don't recall something—does the letter say whose apartment Mr. Noach will live in? I do have certain requirements: no stairs, no...."

Pieretta's hope for finding a legal way out of the enforced meeting was extinguished when Doreen replied, "Um, it's here, at the bottom of the letter. *'Due to your pre-existing medical condition, you will be allowed to remain in your current dwelling. Mr. Noach will move in the day after your first meeting.'* Are you all right? Can I get you something?"

Pieretta creakily shook her head, her thin-lipped mouth moving into a downward-arcing crescent. *Damn them and their "concern" for my well-being.* "I'm fine. Tell me again, what time is this first scheduled 'meeting' of ours?"

"Tomorrow at nine A.M. Um, since you brought it up, I got my own letter from the government—as of the day Mr. Noach moves in, he'll be taking over your caregiving duties. It's designed to encourage bonding."

*Does this man have a job? Do they realize what he's taking on?* Trying to keep her voice even, Pieretta said, "I'm sorry—you were offered another job, I trust? You are set financially, yes?"

"Oh, not to worry. Me and the mister, we're doing fine. I have other clients, so not to worry, Miz P. I just hope everything works out with Mr. Noach. If he was picked to be with you, he has to be right for you. I wouldn't worry none. Like they say, it's for everyone's good."

The woman continued to speak, but Pieretta closed in on herself, cocooned in her carapace of tight, taut flesh, allowing herself only to experience the warmth of the sunlight above her, devoid of any accompanying flesh fantasy.

The envelope from the government had contained a thin pamphlet full of suggestions for making the first meeting between sanctioned sex partners successful and "fulfilling." So, early that morning, Pieretta grudgingly submitted to Doreen's physical ministrations—a bath in scented oils followed by a thorough massage, after which she was helped into what the pamphlet dubbed "enticing" garments: lacy panties, a pushup bra, filmy stockings, a strappy garter belt, and, over those scratchy yet clinging undies, a simple wrap-front robe, belted loosely at the waist. Looking down at herself as she sat before her dressing table while Doreen brushed her chin-length bob of dark honey-gold hair, Pieretta thought that a store-window dummy would look more erotic, more sensual; against her unsupple flesh, the clothes seemed to be wearing *her*, imparting no hint of sexuality, no erotic aura whatsoever. Even the uplifted rounded globes of her breasts looked unreal, more like stones resting in slings of frothy white lace.

Once Doreen was done with her hair, she took up a tube of mascara and began applying the brown-coated wand to Pieretta's eyelashes. With each stroke, Doreen's breath puffed out warm and soft on Pieretta's cheeks. Staring past her caregiver, Pieretta daydreamed of the last time she'd actually had real sex with anyone, in the days before her body began its slow, grating transformation from playfully supple to stilted and stiff.

His name had been Aubin. The surname was lost to her, lost in the haze of those endless, golden days spent in Provence, during her last summer abroad—but she supposed that surnames no longer mattered, in memory. He'd been blond, curly-haired, with a thin small thatch of downy hair between his small-nippled breasts, which matched the tight, small patch of down over his manhood. His hair had tickled her, against her breasts, along her thighs, under her chin as she'd gone down on him and he'd run his fingers through her much longer hair, weaving them through her curls, tugging playfully when she'd used her tongue and teeth. Then, when she was done, and they were lying side by side on that ridiculously lumpy mattress in her motel room, he'd taken the ends of her flowing hair and brushed it against her nipples, until they puckered like sweet pink raisins over her swelling breasts, and then he was kissing her, moving from her lips to her aching nipples, down along her convex belly, until his tongue parted her other lips, and she could feel his curls tickling her lower belly. She'd let out a low, throaty laugh and reached down to massage his sunburned shoulders, pressing him closer to her parted softness.

She'd been so soft, so flexible, then; she and Aubin had slithered snakelike together on the uneven mattress, their bodies shifting and reconfiguring, forming positions of the most complex sexual geometry. In memory, they flowed, sweat-slicked flesh slapping and sucking gently with each movement, each shift against the yielding sheets. As Doreen now smoothed foundation on Pieretta's slack cheeks, the stone-still woman closed her eyes and imagined Aubin's broad palms cradling her face between his hands as he kissed her deeply, his tongue twisting and teasing against hers.

"There we are—all done. Here, take a look." Doreen turned her around to look at her reflection in the vanity mirror.

As long as she concentrated on her hair, which hadn't changed all that much during the long years of her illness, Pieretta could stomach what she saw before her. And her eyes: They were still murky sapphire blue, still what might be called beautiful. Best to concentrate on those two unaltered features, and let her vision glaze over when it came to her angular planed face, the taut lips, the oddly shining skin.

"I think you look stunning. I'm sure Mr. Noach will be most pleased."

"Pleased doesn't have anything to do with it, does it? He has to come here, whether he wants to or not." When she saw the reflected hurt in the caregiver's eyes as she continued to stare past her own image, Pieretta quickly added, "I'm just nervous, please don't mind me. Yes, I'm sure he'll be happy with what you've done for me."

Doreen gave Pieretta's hard shoulders a squeeze before reminding her, "Be sure to take your Thalomid before he gets here. I suspect you two will be quite busy afterward."

Telling herself that the woman really did mean well, Pieretta coaxed her lips into a smile under the coat of pale pink lipstick (specifically suggested in the pamphlet as being more sexually inviting than the traditional red shades), then said, "Oh, I'm sure we will be." She hoped that her voice didn't betray her feelings to the contrary.

The apartment was too quiet, too echoing, as Pieretta waited for Mr. Noach's arrival, but she was loathe to turn on her radio or put some CDs into the changer. She was damned if she'd make things easier for him; true, she'd done what she was tacitly required to do—make her body as clean and tempting as possible—but other than that, Mr. Noach was on his own.

He'd have to be; sex per se had long ago become too diffi-cult, too taxing for her, as she'd so plainly stated on those forms she'd filled out months ago. Eating was difficult enough, let alone giving head, and her body had lost all physical rhythm years ago, to the point where anyone who might be able to put it in her wouldn't get any more response than a blowup doll or a mechanical vagina might offer. Less, probably.

"I hope your wrists are strong. They'll be getting plenty of exercise," she mumbled to herself, seconds before the doorbell chimed. Already standing—the effort of getting in and out of a chair was too exhausting—she forced herself to say loudly, "I'll be there in a minute," then deliberately took a full minute to reach the door and jerk the knob open.

A rush of cool air from the hallway beyond hit her, reflex-ively making her nipples pucker under her flimsy robe; she got her first look at the man the government had chosen as her ideal sexual mate.

He was an old-looking thirty-four. Fine creases ham-mocked his light-brown eyes, and his jawline was already jowly and slack, with the first hint of a double chin. His hair was lightly salted with silver, but still mostly dull brown, cut severely at the nape of the neck and above his ears, but some-what more generously over his wrinkle-banded forehead. His nose was...a nose: not too wide, not too big. Slightly large pores, but his face was clean-shaven, and obviously well-scrubbed.

His envelope had contained a pamphlet too.

Howard Noach was taller than she was, at least five-ten or five-eleven, and, while not buff, he wasn't overly flabby. Average, in virtually all respects—save for his hands, which were far more used-looking than his somewhat bland face and unremarkable body. The whitish scars and thick calluses cou-pled with his roughened webbed flesh spoke of hard, perhaps dangerous work in his past. His hands worked, *hard*. The nails were worn down to the quick, with absolutely no white showing. A small nail-bed, so that each finger was tipped with a tiny hard end, and no more.

Despite her previous trepidation, she wondered what those hands and blunt fingertips might feel like on her skin, and thrust deep within her unyielding inner folds.

He wore the male version of the government pamphlet's suggested sensual clothing: loose-fitting cotton pants, a softly clinging shirt over bare skin, and slip-off shoes. His flesh too had been bath-oiled and cologne-anointed. He'd shaved just that morning; a tiny nick was freshly healed on one cheek.

Turning her attention back to his face, Pieretta noticed that he was smiling, but she wasn't sure if it was from nervousness or pleasure.

"Please, come in. I didn't mean to keep you standing out here."

"Thank you. May I...call you Pieretta? It's such a beautiful name—French, no?"

Nodding as much as she was able, she said, "My mother's French. I used to summer there, when I was in college. Please, sit down."

Mr. Noach hadn't stepped beyond the door, but remained quite still, his hands hanging loosely by his hips. He smiled and said, "No, I'd rather stand, for a while. I'm used to it, from my job."

"Which is...?" Pieretta was momentarily grateful for her condition; back when she was younger, she'd had a habit of rocking from side to side when nervous.

Her new mate rubbed the sides of his legs with his hands, making a gentle susurrus of fabric and flesh that Pieretta found deeply erotic; between her rigid legs she felt a deep, fleshy twinge.

"I'm a sculptor—marble, some stone. When I was in college, I moonlighted as a monument carver: y'know, dates, names on the stones. But my main love is sculpting, figures especially. I guess that's why I was chosen for you. I love figures—looking at them, forming them with my chisel, touching them afterward. They're so still, so...*there*. I like the smoothness that doesn't yield like flesh does. Rubbing my hands over the surfaces, polishing the marble with my palms after the dust's worn away. It gets warm—the marble, the stone. Heat from my hand transfers to the statue, it's beautiful. Those small, warm spots rubbed smooth and slick—better than the women who model for me. Some of them, they're so fleshy soft, they're like dough. And of course, no respectable artist fondles his models—it's unprofessional. God, don't mind my blathering...." Noach's voice was a soft, slightly baritone drone; as he spoke his eyes never left Pieretta's body.

"No, it's OK, I'm interested," she said. "Please, go on." Slowly she moved her stiff fingers into the deliberately loose knot Doreen had tied in her robe's belt. Working one forefinger into the center of the knot, she jerked the belt loose and let it drop to her stockinged feet. Noach's eyes followed the fabric's fall, then moved back up to the narrow swath of parted fabric over her legs and torso. She used her rake-fingered hands to pull open the robe, and said, "I'm not very good at undoing my bra—if you wouldn't mind...."

Covering the distance between them in three quick strides, her new mate stood before her, his chest rising quickly under the silky fine fabric of his shirt, his hard, blunt hands moving slowly, reverently, to first shuck the robe off her shoulders, then gently slide under her arms to reach the hook-and-eyes in back of her bra. The tips of his fingers were pleasantly hard and smooth against her taut back muscles; they unhooked the bra and slid up her shoulder blades to tenderly lift the straps from her shoulders before pulling the bra off her rigid torso in a downward, breast-revealing motion. Pieretta sighed as her eyelids slid closed.

While her breasts had long ago become permanently jutting and what the caregivers affectionately dubbed "perky," her nipples could still react, slowly, but significantly, and as they puckered into tighter nubs in the middle of her areola, she felt the wet heat of Howard Noach's lips and tongue caressing them, gently sucking and kneading with his teeth, his hands moving down her hard, smooth flesh, down her hips, to slide off her garter belt and panties in one shucking motion. The rush of air that tickled her legs as the lacy fabric slipped down her body was intoxicating in its subtlety. Moving his hands in a circular rubbing motion, Howard polished her firm, unyielding skin as if it were the finest marble, leaving patches of hot, sated flesh in his wake.

After he took his mouth from her breasts, exposing the wet flesh to the dry warm air, Howard kissed each of her taut cheeks in turn, whispering, "So still, so stone-still. All my life I wanted someone like you—someone so alive, so still. Before, when I'd try to tell a woman what I wanted, she'd think I was a kink, but it's just something I *like,* so much. What I'd carve could be touched, but it never *cared* whether it was touched or not. I never thought of myself as a freak, I just love touching, and looking. Kneading and manipulating just isn't my thing, I like what's there already. Can you understand that? I'm not some weirdo, I just love *looking, touching*—but not changing a woman. Just looking at the planes of her skin, seeing the light hit it, feeling that smoothness and firmness under my hands. You can't *believe* how that turns me on. But the statues, they didn't radiate warmth back. And the smell is always the same, that clean water-sterile scent, slightly dusty at first, then just clean. But your skin—there's heat, and a tang to the flesh."

He moved his lips close to her ear, under the well-brushed hair, and continued, his words a soft, wind-soothing rush. "Something I couldn't get from the women who posed for me, something that wasn't there in the statues, but something I still *wanted*. When I filled out the forms for the government, I never *dreamed*...I thought they'd toss me aside, consider me unworthy of any match. I never dreamed anyone like you could exist."

Somewhere deep within Pieretta, the memory of Aubin and his tickling pale curls grew faint, faint as a whisper, while the dry heat of her mate's circular caresses whisked away the last echoes of that whisper, in a raspy susurrus of hard flesh meeting harder flesh.

# Tit Man

*Lisa Archer*

"A man with breasts!" I exclaim, sweeping his shirt off his
shoulders to expose his whole chest. He's entirely naked
now. Standing behind his chair, I reach around, running
my hands over the soft breasts beneath sparse, curly chest
hair. His cock strains upward, eagerly emitting a clear
droplet.

Roger has been seeing me since May of '98. He called in
response to an ad I placed in the local weekly.

"What attracted you to my ad?" I had questioned the
soft voice on the phone.

"The fact that you said you were down-to-earth and
kinky." He had asked my hourly fee, then had offered to
pay a generous portion of that amount if I would go on a
coffee date before our first session.

We met on a Wednesday morning at the Dolores Park
Café. I was standing in line for coffee, when a man with
curly gray hair paused just inside the door and glanced
around, scratching his moustache and beard. His eyes,
swimming in far-sighted glasses, finally fixed on me.

"Roger, come join me in line," I called out, as though we'd been friends for years.

Hunched in his tweed jacket, Roger crept up beside me. "Can we get our coffee to go and take a walk in the park?" he asked.

Like most clients I meet in public, he was nervous about being caught—as if our foreheads were blazing with *J* for *john* and *W* for *whore*. The truth is, it takes one to know one. To strangers unfamiliar with the business, such meetings rarely look like anything more racy than a blind date.

Dolores Park, known affectionately to the locals as "the gay beach," swarms with men lying butt naked on the sunny grass. Just downhill, Latina mothers push their squealing children on the swings. The wind swallowed our voices that morning, as Roger and I blended into the odd soup of people. It was, in short, the perfect place to negotiate a trick.

At first we made small talk about what we did when we weren't seeing whores or johns respectively. Roger was a professor of primate biology. Since I was just finishing up a degree in the humanities, we commiserated about petty departmental politics. His words were soft and soothing, though his lips trembled.

Finally, far from the range of potential eavesdroppers, Roger began. "I'm what you'd call an adulterer. I know that, and I admit it. I feel horribly guilty about it, but that doesn't make me stop. I love my wife, but there's no passion in our relationship anymore. We're good friends. She doesn't know about any of this, though." I listened. This was all pretty run-of-the-mill, though most of my clients don't actually refer to themselves as "adulterers."

"Have you had these sorts of arrangements in the past?" I asked.

"Oh, many, over the years."

I cut to the chase. "So what are you looking for?"

"Well," he said, "let me tell you a little about the arrangement that worked best for me. It was with a woman I saw for about four years. We would see each other every two or three weeks, and during those times we spent about an hour-and-a-half together. After she'd known me a couple of years, she said that what I was really into was 'erotic embarrassment.' See, there's a part of my anatomy that's really humiliating for me. As long as I can remember—since I was a little boy—I've had breasts. I was so ashamed of them. The other kids teased me horribly. Even today I wear a jacket most of the time. But over the years I've learned that what really turns me on is to have a woman fondle my breasts and kind of tease me about them. It's terrifically embarrassing, but I get so turned on."

"I can certainly do that," I assured him.

"Well, how would noon tomorrow work for you?"

The next day Roger appeared at my door promptly at twelve o'clock—grinning from ear to ear and toting a wrinkly, white plastic bag from Walgreens.

"What's in the bag?" I asked.

"Well, as I said, I'm a seasoned adulterer. I bring my own shampoo, soap, deodorant, and toothpaste from home, so I won't smell any different after I see you."

He ambled nervously across my living room, glancing about, and finally flopped into a large armchair in the corner.

"Do you mind if I smoke a cigarette?" he asked.

"No, that's OK. I think I have an ashtray in the kitchen." I opened the window beside his armchair and set the ashtray on the ledge.

"I don't usually smoke, but I like to when I do this." He lit his cigarette and took a drag. "I enjoyed our conversation yesterday."

"So did I. Thanks for being specific about what you want. It makes my job a lot easier."

"Oh, I didn't used to be this way at all. It took me years to figure out that this was the only way to do it—years of trial and error." He sank back in his chair and glanced out the window for a few minutes, then said whimsically, "You know, what I'd really like today is for you to discover my breasts. You know, undress me. And, even though you know that I have breasts, act surprised." He stood up facing me. Taking a few steps closer, I slid my hands slowly under the lapels of his jacket and felt the soft lobes of his breasts.

"You do have breasts!" I exclaimed. Smiling mischievously, I opened his jacket. "May I take this off?"

"Yes—please." Roger swallowed hard, fumbling out of the sleeves of his coat. He was wearing a white oxford shirt. I cupped his tits in my hands.

"You have breasts just like a woman's. I bet you wear about a C cup. Have you ever tried on a bra?"

"No, and I have no desire to," he said flatly. I took my hands off his breasts and led him over to a full-length mirror.

"Have a seat." I pulled up a chair facing the mirror. Roger sat down, and together we gazed at ourselves: Roger already blushing and squirming a little, and me standing behind him, resting my hands on his shoulders.

Leaning over, I whispered in his ear, "I've never seen a man with breasts before. I *have* to look at them." I fingered the top buttons of his shirt and slowly unfastened them, whispering: "Look at yourself in the mirror. They're just like a woman's. I've just never seen anything like it before. Look at yourself!"

Three years later, Roger still calls a day in advance to book his noon appointment.

"Are you going running on the beach tomorrow morning?" he asks.

"I think so."

"You won't shower afterward."

"No."

Roger likes to lick the sweat off my chest and armpits. He wants me to greet him at the door in a white tank top and jeans with holes in the crotch and nothing underneath. I smell as if I've been playing in the sand. It reminds him of being a boy in a playground, he says. Sometimes he takes me right then, pushing me up against the wall, pressing his hard meat against my thigh. A condom opens, rolls down his cock, and, knowing that he is only here for an hour, I melt into him, and that moment grows until it fills the whole world, and there is nothing but him inside me and his touch.

He knows I come this way. Simple, easy, and efficient. But Roger doesn't get off by taking me like that. He does it because he wants to watch me come, to know that he can make me come, and that I trust him enough to let go of myself. He also wants to satisfy me in advance, "because you have to work so hard to get me off," he explains.

Roger lies on his back naked. "Oh my God, you have breasts!" I pull his nipples upward and shake his tits. "Look, a man with breasts! Just like a woman's." His cock jumps at the magic words.

I tell Roger stories based on his favorite fantasies. Like many johns I've seen over the years, he likes to believe he's submitting to me, after he gives me precise directions of what he wants me to do. To produce the illusion that I'm actually dominating him, I "make" him lick my pussy and ass-hole while I'm talking.

"We're in a department store. I'm taking you into the women's dressing room. You like that, don't you?"

"Mmm-hmm," he nods.

"The women are changing. We can see their bare ankles under the dressing room doors. I knock on the first door we pass. The woman who opens it is beautiful. She has long, dark hair and gorgeous breasts. You want to touch them, don't you?"

"Yes—please!"

"Not yet. First I have to show her *your* breasts. I unbutton your shirt and make you take it off: 'Look! He has breasts. It's a man with breasts!' Her mouth drops open, eyes widen. I ask her to touch them. She reaches out her hand slowly, tentatively."

"May I touch myself—pleeease?" he pleads.

"Not yet," I say.

Breathing deeply, I switch to a different story.

"I'm taking you to a private party for women. You're the only man here. As we enter the room—full of naked women— I announce that I've brought a man with tits, who's going to be our sex toy for the evening. He's here to serve us all, and anyone can make him do whatever she desires. The women cluster around you, screaming, 'Man with tits! Man with tits!' Dozens of hands reach for you—tearing off your shirt and pulling at your hair. They drag you over to a sling and make you kneel between the legs of one woman after another. You have to service them one by one—licking each woman's pussy and her asshole until she comes five times. Meanwhile the other women fondle and play with your breasts."

Glancing at the clock, I see that we have only fifteen minutes left. "Roger, do you want to come inside me, or jerk yourself off while I play with your breasts?"

He glances up over the curls of my pubic hair: "May I do both? May I please be inside you first?"

Roger's cock curves upward like a devil's tail. I roll the condom down his shaft, take his cock in my hand, and rim the inside of my pussy lips with the head.

He pushes his cock deep inside me.

I grab his nipples, twist them hard, and start telling the story that turns him on most of all.

"I'm a woman executive, dressed in a tailored gray suit. I work in a big, airy office building way up high in a skyscraper, and you're my office slave. There's a knock at the door. It's my personal assistant. She's new in the office and hasn't seen your breasts yet. 'I have something to show you,' I tell her. I stand behind you and unbutton your shirt. She's stunned. 'It's a man with breasts!' 'May I touch them?' She runs her hands over your breasts in disbelief. 'He's here to serve us tea,' I tell her. 'And you can fondle his breasts as much as you want.'"

Roger is panting. He collapses on top of me and starts pumping hard. I can tell he's about to come. I keep talking, raising my voice over his loud breathing.

"I make you take off all your clothes and invite her to sit with me, while you serve us tea. We're seated at a low coffee table, so that you have to lean way over to set the teapot down. As you lean over, your tits hang over the table. We fondle them: 'Look! A man with breasts! Look how his tits dangle when he leans over.'"

"I'm coming—now! Oh, Gaaa!" His body quivers, contracting like a jackknife as he comes. He lets go of me and rolls onto his back, wrapping his arms around his knees. Just when I think he's done coming, he groans again, coiling back into a ball.

At the end of our session Roger heads for the shower as always—to use the shampoo and soap he carries in his Walgreens bag. I sit down beside the coffee table and count the stack of twenties that Roger slipped me at the beginning of our session.

Suddenly something goes thump in the bathroom. I rush down the hall and rap on the door.

"Are you all right?"

"Please, help me!" I push the door open. The metal ring that holds up the shower curtain has fallen. Roger stands in the bathtub, balancing it awkwardly on his shoulders. The scene would be funny, but he's sobbing. The tap is still running, and all I can see through the plastic curtain are trails of blood streaming down his legs.

I grab the metal rod and lift it off him.

"Where are you hurt?"

"I don't know. I slipped. I must have grabbed onto this thing. Then I noticed I was bleeding." There's a patch of blood on his temple, and a steady stream pouring out of a puncture wound and running down his front torso and legs in jagged streaks.

"Is that the only place you're hurt—on your head?"

"I think so."

"Can you get out of the tub?"

"I think so. I think I'm all right." He steps out onto the black bathmat. I hold him by the arms facing me and look into his pupils. They look the same, normal size.

"Do you feel dizzy?"

"No, I'll be all right."

"Did you fall and hit your head?"

"No, I think I just pulled the rod down on my head. I really don't know what happened."

"I want you to lie down on the floor—right side facing up—while I get some ice." I help him lie down, then run down the hall to grab a bag of frozen peas from the freezer. My roommate, who I forgot was home, meets me in the hallway and follows me back to the bathroom.

"What happened?"

"He slipped in the shower."

"Should I call an ambulance?" she asks.

"No—please!" Roger, overhearing us, pleads.

"Roger, I might have to drive you to the emergency room. It's only a few blocks away."

"No!" he cries, curled in a fetal position. "Please, don't!"

"I can stop the bleeding with pressure, but I'm worried you might have a concussion, or need stitches or something."

"I just pulled the thing down on my head! I'm really fine! What will I tell my wife?" he sobs.

My roommate motions me out of the bathroom. "So," she says under her breath, "do you want me to call an ambulance or not?"

"I don't think so—not this second."

"OK," she says hesitantly. "But I need to use the toilet—like now."

"Just a minute." I cover Roger with a beach towel and squat beside him, holding the bag of peas over the wound on his right temple. The blood has already pooled under his head.

My roommate tiptoes around him. "Geez, that's a lot of blood."

After she leaves, I lift the towel and wipe the streaks of blood off Roger's belly and legs with a wet sponge. Roger is shaking. I wring the sponge out in the tub. Watery blood oozes over my knuckles.

"Oh, God! What am I going to tell her?" he sobs. For the past three years we've played with shame. But this is the first time I'm seeing Roger's shame head-on—his shame about cheating on his wife and being brought into the emergency room and exposed as a man with tits who sees whores.

"What am I going to tell her?" he sobs again.

"We'll think of something," I say, calmly as I can. "Why don't you say you hit your head on the corner of the car door? Or how about falling in your own shower? Is your wife home today?"

"No, she's not."

"Well, do you ever go home from work during the day?"

"Sometimes."

We don't end up at the emergency ward after all. After about forty minutes, the bleeding stops. By that time I've wiped most of the blood off Roger's body. He dresses, thanks me profusely, and declines offers of assistance, assuring me that he can drive home safely: It's only a few minutes away. He leaves, holding a damp wad of Kleenex and a fresh bag of frozen peas on his head.

I escort him to the door and hug him goodbye. "Please call me tomorrow morning and let me know you're OK."

The next morning he calls.

"Roger, how are you?"

"I'm fine now. I ended up going to a clinic. When I got back from your place, I took a shower, and I started bleeding all over again. So I had to go through the whole thing again—putting pressure on it to stop the bleeding. That took about forty-five minutes. Finally I drove myself to a clinic to get it checked out. They gave me two stitches on the head and said I was fine."

"So did you tell your wife you'd fallen in your own shower?"

"Oh, that's all fine too. She didn't think anything of it."

"I'm glad things turned out OK."

"I am, too." He pauses. "Say," he asks casually. "Do you have any appointments at noon today?"

# The Man in the Gray Flannel Tights
*Susan St. Aubin*

All day at work, Hal fantasized about change, even though he was continually changing jobs, moving from company to company as they went out of business, or reorganized their computer divisions, or bought new software he scorned, or tried to impose dress codes on him. The minute a boss said ties on Mondays, jeans only on Fridays, Hal was ready to move on. There was always a friend who knew of an opening or was starting up something new. His life was change, yet change made it the same.

Evelyn was still his wife, even though neither of them spent much time at home and often saw each other only in passing. As he left for an early-morning run, she would be coming in from a night of baking for the restaurant where she worked, or maybe a night with the boyfriend he knew about or one of the girlfriends he didn't want to know about, whose images flickered at the place where his mind froze. Marian was still his girlfriend but didn't have much time for him now that she'd switched from teaching kindergarten part-time to a full-time job teaching art as well as heading the whole arts program at the local high school. She'd become someone he saw from a distance, like his wife, both of them spinning away from him.

As time passed and jobs changed, Friday attire slipped from jeans to loose T-shirts and baggy khakis or shorts. There *is* no style any more, thought Hal, by which he meant no sex—the women's clothes were as shapeless as the men's. T-shirts occasionally slipped to reveal the shadow of a breast, but hips remained hidden beneath shorts that bagged over their knees, or pants that drooped at the waist and bunched around the ankles.

He was shocked to realize that he was getting old enough to remember a different style. Only a few years ago women had worn tights. Some still did—well-toned women in their early forties coming out of gyms—but not the women he worked with, not Evelyn, who now wore the loose white drawstring pants of restaurant workers, and certainly not Marian, who had always favored long, shapeless dresses to hide the wonderfully full hips she seemed ashamed to show. It occurred to him that if he wore what he wanted to see, others might copy him, starting a trend more to his liking. He didn't think men had ever worn tights, except maybe bike riders. He went to sporting goods stores to try on bicycle pants, but they were rubbery and heavy, with stripes in lurid shades running down the legs. When Hal took them off, they crackled like shrink-wrap, an implied kinkiness that disturbed him.

"Did you ever wear tights?" he asked Marian one Tuesday night in May after dinner at her house. He knew what the answer would be, but he wanted to prod her.

She was standing at the sink in the kitchen area of her studio apartment, her back to him so that he could see her shoulders stiffen. "Not me, no, they never fit right. I don't have the figure for them," she said as she rinsed their plates.

He thought she was wrong, and his cock stirred as he pictured her full hips in tights, black tights with a tight white top. He had to cross his legs to compress his erection. They'd had sex before dinner, which was Marian's limit; anything more would be excessive. He thought fondly of Evelyn, whom he could lure into bed (or on the floor or the kitchen table) anytime. The fact was, he had more fun with his wife, and often wondered, when he was with Marian, why he was there.

"Do men ever wear tights?" he asked. He expected a sensible answer guaranteed to put the idea of tights out of his head, but Marian surprised him.

"Dancers," she answered. "Ballet and modern. But then, dancers have the body. You have to have the right body, slender yet muscular."

She had a dreamy look he found promising, as though she were watching dancing men, but he knew bodies were just raw material to her, shapes to be arranged artistically in space—a line here, a curve there.

"Bike riders," she continued, looking out the window over her sink at the brick wall opposite. "But they're so sporty that what they wear doesn't seem like tights."

"They have legs like sticks," Hal agreed.

Marian turned around to say, "Shakespeare. Robin Hood." She began to laugh. "Men used to be the ones who wore tights."

"So how'd women get into them?" He liked the way this conversation was drifting. "How come women took over the tights?"

Marian shrugged as she turned back to the dishes.

"I want tights," Hal said, so abruptly he startled himself. He watched the muscles of her back jump beneath the thin T-shirt she wore over her long skirt. "I want to take back the tights!" he whooped, laughing.

Marian didn't turn around, because the thought of a man in tights made her blush and she didn't want Hal to take this as approval. His birthday was next week, and tights occurred to her as a good surprise for him. Such a gift seemed more like something Evelyn would come up with, and Marian wanted to unsettle her, maybe even alarm her. She often felt Evelyn didn't take her seriously enough to feel threatened. But tights! Who would ever suspect that Marian would think of men in tights? She savored the thought of Evelyn's jealousy. She imagined dancers again; she liked ballet, and, more secretly, she admired the muscular legs, the intriguing bulges, of male dancers, whose discretely bound genitals seemed no more than an extra muscle tamed beneath the fabric of their tights.

Marian ran more hot water into the sink, plunging her hands in steaming suds. Her ears, she knew, were now bright red. If Hal noticed, she wanted the heat of the water as an excuse, but to her relief, he lounged on her bed with the newspaper and began reading an article to her about the stock market.

"Technology, that's where the real future is. Forget everything else," he said.

Marian wondered whom she could ask about tights, and realized that Evelyn was probably the only person who might know where men's tights could be found. Only Evelyn would understand her attraction to tights, and the thought that she had possibly already bought him a pair made Marian angry enough to drop a glass against the sink's rim, where it shattered into the water in hundreds of slivers. Hal leaped off the bed and ran to her, holding her in his arms while she sucked a spot of blood off a small cut at the tip of her left index finger.

"You'd better drain this water," said practical Hal. "Then I can get all the glass out."

His jeans, when he bent over the sink, were tight as a dancer's leotards. *Ballet ass*, she thought. *I'm inventing sexual terms. Ballet ass.* Delighted, she put her hands over her mouth. This was a secret she could keep from Hal and Evelyn both. She liked the double meaning of *ass,* especially appropriate now because Hal was being such an ass, warning her to be more careful when she washed dishes. He was like a scolding mother, cautiously picking glittering slivers from the sink's trap as though he were plucking diamonds from mud, and setting them carefully on the counter.

Now that Marian was an art teacher, people made assumptions about her, often telling her things she'd rather not know concerning their sex lives and drug habits. They shared suspicions with her about who might be gay, or having an affair, as well as envious comments about what they thought of as her bohemian lifestyle. Sometimes Marian wanted to be deaf, to be able to nod politely in response to mouthings she couldn't understand and to communicate with others like herself in a secret language of signs.

On Wednesday as she sat in the teacher's break room, Marian thought of someone else she could ask about tights— Ed, who taught journalism and was gay, though no one suspected, not with his deep voice and dominant manner. Ed made assumptions about Marian, too, and when no one was around, he would tell her about the guys in the gym where he worked out, and about Sunday afternoons in the bushes of the local park, behind the playground there, and he'd say she'd never guess what went on there. One day, he'd even brought up the subject of women's dress sizes.

"I'm sure you've noticed," he'd said as he raised his arms to flex his well-developed muscles, "the more expensive the dress, the smaller the size. A boy just can't tell what size will fit! It's so confusing, because men's clothes run just the opposite. Men want to be big."

While waiting for Ed to come in, Marian unwrapped her cheese sandwich and listened to Jill, the home economics teacher.

"Ed just exudes masculinity," she whispered. "I can't believe he's still single."

"I don't think he is, exactly," Marian muttered to her bread. Jill looked at her, waiting for the wisdom Marian was too discreet to impart. Charm run amok was Ed's defense. With his narrow, deep-blue eyes, short well-styled hair, and the tight dark turtleneck sweaters that set off his muscles, he couldn't possibly be that object of Jill's frequently expressed frustration, the gay man. Marian also knew he dyed his hair, **though this was the one thing he hadn't confessed to her,** because she recognized the color as the exact shade of brown her mother used.

"It's hard to meet men these days," Jill lamented. "It seems like everyone's gay or married, except Ed."

Marian mumbled, "I haven't noticed," while smoothing her long skirt. She pictured herself as a nun, her black wimple falling in folds over her body, like the teachers she'd had in Catholic grade schools, an image that stayed with her as she got off the couch to talk to Ed when he came in.

"Do you know," she asked softly as they sat side by side in two hard teacher's desk chairs, "where a man could buy tights?"

"Anyone we know?" He looked around the room. Jill tried to catch his eye, but he turned his glance back to Marian. "Is he a dancer?"

"No, just a man who wants to wear tights."

Ed's eyebrows shot up. "A small man?" He leaned forward, chin on his knuckles.

"Tall," replied Marian. "Not big, but very tall."

"Let me think. I could suggest a theatrical costume store, but they're expensive, especially tall sizes. What he needs is large women's sizes."

"Large?"

"Yes, sizes for *big* women. You know, 1X, 2X, 3X. Many men find these sizes fit them very well. With a tall man, the legs might be a bit short, but with tights, it's all in how you stretch the fabric."

Marian covered her mouth and smiled. "I can't believe we're talking about men in women's tights right here in the teacher's lounge," she whispered.

"It's not unheard of, in drama classes," he said. In addition to journalism, Ed taught an occasional drama course because the school didn't have a drama teacher yet. "We bought some X-size tights for the guys just last year, when we did *Romeo and Juliet.*"

Marian's heart pounded and her ears burned. Jill winked and waved at her. Ed patted her knee before he stood up, stretched, and moved to the couch.

"What am I going to do, surrounded as I am all day with so many beautiful ladies?" He sat down beside Jill. "What if I lose control? What kind of example would that be for the boys?"

The store Ed recommended was one that everyone called the Fat Lady Store in the mall, though it was really Splendid Fantasy: Clothes for Women, and had a picture painted over the entrance of a not so very large woman in harem pants and a bangled headdress holding a golden oil lamp in both hands. Marian hummed along with the music the piano player under the dome at the center of the mall was playing as she strolled inside on Saturday morning, armed with her new knowledge of X sizes. She half expected to see Evelyn, who surely knew how to clothe men in large women's tights, beating her to the surprise gift—but the shop was empty, with only one saleswoman, possibly a size 14, standing behind a counter shuffling price tags like cards.

"May I help you?" she asked without raising her head.

Marian looked around at the racks of dresses and loose jackets, at shelves of hats and wide-sized shoes. She picked up the sleeve of one dress, size 12, and dropped it as though it burned her fingers. The price was $350. Was it made of silk? Cashmere? Woven gold? Marian was a size 12. All along, this store she never went to had been for her, because she was beginning to be fat, she and the woman behind the counter, who now raised her eyes to look at her. Marian's eyes were fixed on a row of her favorite long, loose dresses.

"Tights," she murmured. "Where would I find tights?"

The saleswoman sniffed. "Oh, we're not wearing those this year." Her voice lowered with the confidential tones of fashion expertise. "Last year, yes, we did carry them. But now...." She turned to a rack of clothes so new they didn't have price tags yet. "These are what we're wearing these days. I think this would be your size."

She spread a pair of baggy drawstring pants, size 12, in beige raw silk, on the counter.

Marian's fingers reached out to stroke the fabric. "Actually, I'm looking for something for a friend," she said. "A friend who wears a larger size." The saleswoman sucked in her breath as she pulled the silk pants away from Marian. "What size?" she asked.

"X," answered Marian, who found herself not quite remembering what Ed had told her. "I think—2X?"

"Yes, we carry that size," said the woman, as her hands emerged from under the counter with another pile of beige silk to spread out before Marian, who tried to picture Hal swathed in this material, perhaps drowned in it. The clerk smoothed the pants with her hands while Marian reached out a forefinger. She didn't own anything silk, a luxury she couldn't allow herself as long as there were people in the world who didn't have enough to eat.

"How much?" she asked.

"Two fifty," the woman answered, a price that took Marian a moment to digest. Dollars? Hundreds? She pulled her finger back.

"I really was looking for tights," she said.

The clerk sighed. "As I said, we don't carry those." She began putting the silk pants on hangers. "You could try Macy's. Or even the Emporium might...." Her voice trailed off as she looked away from Marian, who felt herself condemned to fashion hopelessness. The clerk's silence followed her out the door.

In the Women's Department in a dark corner of the Emporium's basement, Marian stood by a rack of tights. 1X, 2X, 3X: She held each size up to compare it to the others. Size 2X seemed to have the longest legs, size 3X the widest waist. 1X didn't seem much larger than her own size 12, though it was hard to tell with tights, which would stretch much more than her size 12 jeans. Here in the Women's Department there were no size 12s, or even 14s or 16s. This was X territory, filled with dresses Marian could wrap around herself three times, as well as piles of tights and racks of enormous shirts with sleeves that hung to Marian's knees when she held them in front of her.

She wondered why whoever designed these clothes figured heavy women would also have longer legs and arms. Did they conceive of large women's sizes as being for women who were in all senses large, rather than just overweight? Did they in fact design these things with men in mind? She found a blue-and-gray striped shirt that would look good on Hal, and held it up against a pair of tights, size 2X, in gray cotton that was soft and napped like flannel. If he wanted tights, he'd need something to wear with them that would cover his crotch. She looked at the floor, feeling her face flush at the thought of Hal's prick bulging under the tights, barely contained by the thinly stretched gray flannel. He'd wear a jockstrap, of course, thought Marian, pulling away from the fantasy. Surely he already had one; she wouldn't want to buy *that* for him. She imagined everything pushed into a neat bundle, like a purse, covered by the blue-and-gray striped shirt, hidden but available to those who knew what was there.

She carried her finds to the cashier, a small, bored high school girl whom she recognized, who took them out of her hands and pulled off the price tags. $14.99 for the tights, $15.99 for the shirt, two bargains that together came to about a tenth of the price of those silk drawstring pants Marian still coveted for herself. The cashier stuffed them into a bag without looking at Marian, and then, perhaps remembering some part of her training, smiled at the bag as she said, "Have a nice day."

When Hal looked out the small window on his front door, he saw Marian standing there clutching a package to her breast. It was a Friday, the restaurant's busiest night, so Evelyn wouldn't be home for hours. As he opened the door, Marian stepped back, hiding her gift behind her. He blinked at the light from the setting sun, which he found intense after working at his computer in the windowless closet he used for a study.

"Is this a bad time?" she asked.

"No, no, I just wasn't expecting you. Come in, come in." He'd read somewhere that when people don't mean what they say, they tend to repeat themselves, which made him conscious of his words. In fact, he wasn't sure what he meant, since in spite of his desire for change, he often had trouble adjusting to the unexpected.

He felt a moment of something like fear pass through him when he noticed the package. Marian had never before dared to give him a gift—in fact, on her birthday, she'd told him it wasn't right for him, a married man, to give her a present that wasn't also from Evelyn, a notion that struck him as so odd while at the same time sweetly innocent that he'd declared they didn't need to give gifts because they were each other's gift. Now he felt like hugging her and patting her hips in the jeans she wore so rarely that he got excited whenever he saw them, but instead he pointed at the thing she held in front of her, muttering, "What's that?"

She held out her crushed package, wrapped in white paper she'd painted herself with a design of candles and sparklers.

"Happy birthday," she said, with a smile that began with a reluctant twitching at the corners of her mouth. "How does it feel to be 42?"

"I don't know," he replied. "Just like 41, I suppose, but it's only been two days." He backed into his dark hallway, repeating, "Come in, come in. It's OK, Evelyn's at work."

She followed him down the long hall, a dark living room on the left, a dining room connected to it with sliding doors, and on the right the bedroom and, further back, a kitchen and the large hall closet that was Hal's study. Hal went to the living room, drew the blinds, then switched on a floor lamp. Marian trailed behind him holding his gift, until he turned around and took it from her. He sat on the couch, patting the cushion beside him, urging Marian to sit, and, when she did, patted her knee with his left hand while opening the package one-handed, being careful not to tear the paper. When the clothes spilled onto the floor, he bent to retrieve them.

"Tights!" He held them up, letting the legs fall to the floor. "Honest to God! Tights." He squeezed her shoulders and kissed her lightly on the lips. "And what—a shirt?" He unfurled that, too.

"Something to wear with the tights," she explained.

"I'll try them on right now." He stripped off his jeans, underwear, and T-shirt.

"Shouldn't you wear something underneath?" she asked as she watched him pull on the tights.

He stopped. "Should I? I thought tights were underwear. Do women wear anything underneath?"

"Of course," answered Marian, who always wore underpants beneath her pantyhose.

"They don't look like they do, at least not the women I've seen." Hal pulled the tights up to his waist, watching Marian's face as she looked him up and down, her lips pressing together while a blush spread over her cheeks.

The fit was perfect—a bit loose in the legs, perhaps, compared to the way tights fit women, but long enough, and snug enough through the pelvis to nicely contain his bulging crotch. He jumped up and down, laughing as she turned away.

"I like them, I've never felt anything so comfortable," he said, raising a leg to prove his point. He unfolded the shirt and slipped it on, but hesitated when he began to button it. "The buttons are on the wrong side. This is a women's shirt."

"They're women's tights, too," said Marian.

"That's different. They don't make tights for men. But why buy me a women's blouse?"

She shrugged. "I didn't know it would matter. It was there, and it matched the tights."

"I still think I'd rather wear a man's shirt. Wait." He ran across the hall to the bedroom and came back wearing a black T-shirt that didn't quite cover his crotch.

"How about this?" he asked, prancing before her, his penis wobbling inside the tights, which were beginning to stretch out more.

She put both hands over her reddening ears as she laughed. "But that shirt doesn't cover you. You look, you look—"

"Obscene?" he asked hopefully. "Yes! That's my ambition, to be an obscene old man. I'm looking forward to being *sixty-two in tights!*" He was delighted that demure Marian had unexpectedly given him tights. What next? Anything seemed possible. He slid onto the couch beside her, squeezed her shoulders again, then began unbuttoning her blouse.

"No," she said. "This is your house. Evelyn's house. I couldn't."

"Evelyn's at work." He went on unbuttoning her blouse. "Evelyn wouldn't object. You know we both have lovers, but you've never accepted that about Evelyn and me. Evelyn won't mind, she won't know."

Marian sat still as he undid the last button.

"I want you in my house," he whispered in her ear, sucking the lobe while his fingers began working at the button on her jeans.

She breathed rapidly as she wrapped her arms around her open blouse, but she didn't protest when he unzipped her jeans and pulled them off her hips, or when he lowered his lips to the clit protruding pink from a weave of soft brown hair, or when his wet and twisting tongue began its slow massage.

Were her hands on his head, in his hair? Her touch was so tentative he couldn't be sure this wasn't something he was imagining. His hands were kneading her thighs; her juices, mingled with his saliva, ran down his chin. Yes, her hands were fluttering in his hair. When he felt his prick lift the fabric of his tights, he had an image of an enormous stretch, an Aubrey Beardsley lithograph of a giant penis bursting out like a glorious flag, unfurling and waving at Marian.

When Marian's hips rose from the couch, he stuffed his nose into her cunt until she sighed and fell back again, her legs collapsing on either side of his head, her body immobilized with pleasure. Suddenly her hands were on his hair again, this time to push him away. He got up and sat beside her, licking his lips, then kissed her. She turned her head away.

"I never meant for this to happen." She was saying what he knew she thought she should say, although he didn't think she sounded regretful. He missed Evelyn, who cried out as she came, and kicked her legs in the air. Already Marian was standing, pulling on her jeans, buttoning her blouse.

"Wait," he said.

"Oh, no, really, I should go. It's getting late."

"It's only nine. Evelyn won't be home for hours."

But she was leaving him hard beneath his tights, throbbing, congested—leaving him to his own hands, or to Evelyn if he could wait that long.

"So was this shirt a mistake? Would you wear it, or should I take it away?" She looked to the side rather than directly at him, not wanting to see the way his cock made a tent at the crotch of his tights.

"Take it." He looked down at that ridiculous penis pushing at his tights, refusing to either burst through or go away. Evelyn called it the Herald, for big Hal, she said. Herald of what? He willed it to collapse.

Marian picked up the paper from the floor, and wrapped it around the shirt.

"You could wear it," he suggested, but she shook her head.

"It's way too big. I'll have to take it back."

He followed her into the hall and turned on the light. Her hand was on the doorknob.

"Really, I should go."

As he approached her, his tent pole rising again beneath the tights, she stood on tiptoe, bending above the waist to kiss him on the lips, so light and nice that his heart and cock both softened, leaving him with a fatherly tenderness for her. He wanted her here, now, in his living room, and yet he would let her go because she'd brought him a gift, because she was so very nice. He kissed her again on the forehead, whispering, "Your place, a week from this Tuesday, OK?"

"Yes," she murmured, "of course," and was out the door as though she'd never come. He watched her back, which was unexpectedly slender and vulnerable when set off by her sturdy hips in jeans that fit closely without being tight.

He had only the tights to prove she'd been there. He slipped one hand into the waistband, stroking himself as he walked into the living room and sat down on the couch. He pulled the tights down to his ankles, letting his cock free except for his confining hand, but, on the verge of coming, he stopped. She wasn't here, she'd left, why bother? He lay on his back on the couch and watched poor Herald fall in the diffuse light coming from the hall, then pulled up the tights. His eyes felt scratchy when he closed them, and all his muscles went limp.

When he opened his eyes again, Evelyn was tiptoeing around the room. She switched on the lamp by the couch.

"Are you awake? What's this? Tights? You have tights on!" She pulled the waistband, looked in, then let it snap against his stomach. "Where'd you find tights?" She bent over and kissed him, her tongue slowly swirling on his lips. "Hmmm," she murmured, "I sense you have not been alone."

He got up off the couch, saying nothing.

"You're always so mysterious." She laughed as she came up behind him, her hands moving over his ass. As soon as his pole stirred, Evelyn's fingers were on it.

"I've been saving them for you," he said.

She circled him, inspecting the tights. When she crouched in front of him and pulled them down, his cock jumped out.

"Come on, who gave you these tights? It couldn't have been Marian. Who else is there? Men don't just go out and find their own tights."

Her mouth was on him, sucking him into her throat, blowing him out, then sucking him in again. He was tempted to spill sperm and information together, to surprise her with the fact that it *was* Marian who'd bought them, but he didn't, holding back without a word while she worked on him, sucking and squeezing his balls, then his prick, then his balls again until he burst into her mouth and she drank him down. He felt like a good host worrying about the guest who'd left without dessert. Poor Marian, she'd gotten nothing.

Evelyn was chuckling. "My, that was enough for two women, at least. Come on, tell me." She sniffed the tights.

"These are brand new. Unused. You got them tonight, didn't you?"

He leaned against the wall, saying nothing.

"A dancer!" Evelyn pulled his tights up. "She's an exotic dancer and she found these for you backstage, in a bin, new tights for the chorus of boys who dance behind her in her act." She was making up a story for him, as she often did.

"Dance!" she ordered, pulling him away from the wall. "Dance for me."

When she released his arm he spun like a puppet, then put one foot awkwardly up in the air, toes curled. With both feet together on the ground he bounced in place, first springing to the right, then to the left.

Evelyn applauded. "Dance, dance!" she chanted. His cock bobbed up and down beneath the tights as he jigged in time to Evelyn's clapping hands. This was the real thing, he thought, as he felt another tent form in the crotch of his tights. Evelyn, he knew, had just begun with him—so why was he still thinking of Marian's back as she walked down the front steps?

# The Lindy Shark

*Alison Tyler*

With a blare from the slide trombone, Lilly Faye and her Fire-Spittin' Fellas lit into the first number of the evening. Clara rushed to find her place, her polka-dotted dress swirling about her. Within moments she was grabbed around the waist, pulled into a tight embrace, twirled fiercely and without finesse, and then passed to the next man in line. This one had thick, meaty fingers that held her too tightly, creasing the fabric of her carefully ironed dress. She was relieved to be released to the next partner. Her ruffled red panties briefly showed as the third man spun her, dipped her, and passed her on again.

Aside from the briefest of observations, she hardly had time to notice what her partners looked like. Her appraisals were cut short with every turn, only to start fresh with the next. Even when a man did please her, there was no way to act on the attraction. The leader would call out to switch, and she'd be pressed onto the next dancer. Still, she couldn't help but feel a wash of anticipation at the dim prospect that she would be matched with someone who not only suited her moves but also passed her stringent critique system. Although it hadn't happened lately, that didn't mean it couldn't. Maybe *he* would be here again. Perhaps he would notice her this time.

To the sounds of "Jump, Jive, and Wail," Clara found herself with five different men in a row who failed to please her. Handsome, but a poor dancer. Fine looking, but much too short. Sweaty. A groper. Bad, bad hair. Then, finally, as the leader called out for only the experienced lindy-hoppers to take the floor, she saw *him*. She watched him move through the crowd with that insolent look on his face. He had heavy-lidded eyes, a tall, sleek body. Like a shark on the prowl, he cut cleanly through the waves of dancers.

"Fine threads," a woman next to Clara said, staring at the man. "Racket jacket, pulleys, and a dicer," she added.

A little too "in the lingo," thought Clara as she refocused on her dream man—but the woman was right. His vintage zoot suit looked as if it had been tailor-made for him, the suspenders flashed when his coat opened, and the fedora added to his high-class appearance. He had an unreadable expression on his face, a steady gaze that almost seemed to look through her. Then he lifted his chin in her direction, letting her know that he had seen her and approved.

Of course he approved, thought Clara. Her sunset-colored hair, dark red streaked with gold and bronze, was done in pin curls that had taken hours to achieve. She'd applied make-up in the fashion of the era—bright matte lips and plenty of mascara. Her vintage dress was navy with white polka dots, and it cinched tightly around her tiny waist. A pair of stacked heels sturdy enough to dance in, but high enough to make her moves look even more complicated than they were, completed her outfit. She waited for him to come to her side. The girls nearby twittered in hopes that he was coming for one of them.

"I'd let him into my nodbox," one murmured.

Clara agreed: She'd definitely let this man crease her sheets. She felt like telling the giggling women to give up—the man didn't have eyes for any of them. He was on his way to Clara.

A rush of nervous excitement pulsed between her legs and flooded outward. Rarely did she feel this self-conscious—normally her moves expressed a quality that came from within, a radiance on the dance floor that couldn't be taught. This man possessed it too—that's what attracted her. Dancing could be a form of foreplay; she'd always known that. But at most of these swing sessions, there simply wasn't anyone she wanted to take to bed. Sure, she was picky when it came to men— both as dance partners and bed partners. That wasn't a crime, was it? If you chose the right person, for either activity, the results were much more satisfying.

The man reached her side just as a new song began. He didn't say a word, simply put one hand on her waist and steered her onto the floor.

She took her time checking him out. Up close, he was even more attractive. Those dark liquid eyes, like a silent film star's, were infinitely expressive. A deep inky blue, they shone beneath the crystal chandelier. His hands were large and firm, and they maneuvered her with expertise, without roaming where they didn't belong. That was a surprise. Men often took the opportunity to fondle a partner, something Clara generally found distasteful. Now she wouldn't have minded if his hands wandered down a bit, if he tried a little stroking as they glided together on the dance floor.

Clara usually didn't have to think while she danced—her feet easily followed her partner's lead. But this man was making her work, executing several difficult steps from the very beginning, forcing her to concentrate. She forgot about what she hoped he might do to her and focused on keeping up with him.

Other dancers spread out to give them room, as if they sensed something big about to happen. And it was. As the first song blended into a second, and then a third, the duo found their zone. When her partner flipped her into the air, Clara let out a happy little squeal, something totally out of character for her. For the first time, the man smiled. It was as if a marble sculpture had cracked. For the rest of the dance, the moves came naturally. Clara no longer had to second-guess him, to think about where he was going. Instinctively, she followed.

When the music stopped so that Lilly Faye and her Fellas could take a breather, Clara kept following him—down the hallway from the main ballroom and into a small, unisex bathroom. This wasn't something she would normally do, but if he could dance like that, she thought, just imagine how he might make love. He locked the door behind them.

They could hear music drifting in from the ballroom—someone had put on a CD by Big Bad Voodoo Daddy, and it was loud. People headed out to the bar, and voices lifted as spirits flowed. Alcohol mixed with dancing could make people rowdy. Clara was relieved not to be out there with the throng making small talk.

The man lifted her up; she kicked out her heels automatically, as if he was still dancing with her. He wasn't. He set her down on the edge of the blue-and-white tiled sink and cradled her chin in one hand. His full mouth, almost indecently full for a man, came closer. Kissed her. Shivers ran through her body; she closed her eyes and floated on his kiss, not noticing when his fingers moved to the front of her dress and undid the tiny pearl buttons, buttons it had taken her ten minutes to fasten. She remembered standing in her bedroom, looking at her reflection, wondering if this man would be present tonight, if he would like what she was wearing.

Beneath the vintage dress she wore a modern, underwire lace bra and matching panties in crimson silk. The man stroked her breasts through the bra before unfastening the clasp and letting the racy lingerie fall to the floor. When she opened her eyes, she saw their reflection in the mirror across the room. They appeared dream-like, a perfect match. The way it was meant to be.

The man took off his hat and set it on the counter. Then he tilted his head and watched her as she slid out of her dress to stand before him in her ruffled panties, garters, hose, and shoes. Though he didn't speak, he seemed to want her to leave the stockings on. Quickly he turned her so that they faced the mirror above the sink. He lowered her underpants and waited for her to step out of them. She watched in the mirror as he undid his slacks and opened them. She caught a flash of polka dot boxer shorts that matched her dress—another indication of how perfect they were together.

He leaned against her, the length of his cock pressed to the skin of her heart-shaped ass. The silk of his boxers brushed the backs of her thighs, and she sighed. He gripped her waist, letting her feel just how ready he was. His cock was big and hard, and it moved forward, seeking its destination. Without a word, he slipped it between her thighs, probing her wetness. She'd gotten excited during their dancing; her slick pussy lips easily parted and he slipped inside. Just the head. Just a taste.

The band started up in the other room, and, to the lindy beat, he began to fuck her. Clara felt as if they were still dancing. Making love to him was as natural as having him flip her in the air and twirl her around. She opened to his throbbing sex, and to the insistent beat of the music.

The bathroom's art deco style created a fantasy-like atmosphere, with its blue-toned mirror and tiled walls that echoed her sighs. Though he remained silent, the man seemed pleased by the way she moved, rocking her body back and forth, urging him to deeper penetration. He locked eyes with her in the mirror and, for the second time that evening, smiled. It began at the corners of his mouth and moved up to sparkle in his eyes. An intense connection flowed hot between them; she had been right to wait for him. She felt a sense of destiny as he slid his hands up her bare arms, stroking her skin, sending tremors through her body.

She liked the silence, their lack of words. Some boys talked through the whole thing, ruining it. Lovemaking, Clara felt, shouldn't be full of chitchat. She craved mystery, magic—and with him she had it. She felt the same way dancing. Some men talked when they danced, but if you danced well together, you could have an entire conversation without once opening your mouth.

This man seemed to know that. He understood. Not saying a word as he filled her with his cock, he held her gaze, trailing his fingers across her breasts, pinching her nipples between his thumb and forefinger, making her moan and arch her body.

Oh, yes, this was the way to do it, to the sounds of music, in dim twinkling light. She strove to reach climax in synchronicity with him. She squeezed him tightly with her inner muscles, watching his face for a reaction.

His eyes closed, long lashes dark against pale skin, strong jaw set as he held her tight. Yes, it was going to happen. Now. She closed her eyes, as pulses of pleasure flooded through her, gripping onto the edge of the sink to hold herself steady.

After he came he didn't withdraw, but remained inside her, growing hard again almost instantaneously. She sighed with pleasure as he extended the ride, this time taking her harder, faster. She felt as if she might literally dissolve with pleasure. Her senses were heightened, and when he brought one hand between her legs, plucking her clit with knowledgeable fingers, she came, biting her bottom lip hard to keep from screaming. She felt weightless, as she had when he'd tossed her into the air. When she looked in the mirror, she seemed transformed, a flush in her cheeks, a glow in her eyes.

She expected him to be transformed as well. After something so spectacular, shouldn't he be? But when he got dressed he hardly looked rumpled at all, his shirt still cleanly pressed, the fine crease on his pants in place. She felt suddenly exposed, with her bra and panties on the floor, her dress a puddle of polka dots. It would take a bit of work for her to sort herself out. He seemed to understand this, and gave her a final kiss and a wink, and then nodded with his head for her to put on her clothes.

He would meet her outside, she guessed, as she watched him leave, and then hurried to lock the door behind him, her heart pounding like the drum section of Lilly Faye's band. Her fingers trembled as she rebuttoned her dress, taking longer than it had earlier in the evening. She kept mis-buttoning and starting again, desperate to finish so that she could get back out on the floor and dance with him again.

Back in the ballroom, she was certain he would hurry to her side, would lift her up in the air again so that her dress would twirl the way it was meant to. Her crimson ruffled panties would show, and the scent of sex would waft around her like perfume. From now on, they would be partnered, showing off for the rest of the crowd. They would go back to her place that night, and in the morning she would take him to her favorite vintage store on Third Avenue. Would try on clothes for him. Would let him dress her. There were so many things they could do together.

But when she exited the rest room and saw him standing by the wall, he didn't seem to notice her. His eyes roamed over the crowd. She was about to wave her hand, to call out that she was right here, ready to dance. Then she noticed that the two women who'd stood next to her earlier were now at the bar across the way, and the man was heading in their direction. One of the girls let out a high, flirtatious laugh. The man adjusted his suspenders in a practiced, casual manner and tilted his hat forward rakishly.

The room blurred before Clara. She saw the truth. Like a shark, he was moving again through the water of the dancers. After another kill.

# The Flight of the Elephant
## Claudia Salvatori

Two hours on the train, and then two more in line to get into the club—what a hassle. But it's worth it for an excellent night of dancing.

I came with two guys and a girl. One of them, a guy about thirty-five years old, an "unemployed lover of DJs" like in the Marco Masini song, wears a bandana like Vasco Rossi and calls himself a fascist; he gets all excited about Nietzsche's superman and all that junk. He talks to me the whole time about Ezra Pound as if he were his brother. The girl is totally hot, with long, luxurious black hair and two big mama's tits, but she acts like a man. She smokes in the no smoking area and doesn't give a shit, kicks her army boots against the seats, spits on the floor, and rocks back and forth holding onto the railings. She has a little sparkling button in her left nostril, and I know she has another one (she showed it to me) in her clit; she said that getting pierced down there was like having an orgasm times a thousand. I try to imagine what this cyborg sexuality must be like, with artificial members that extend and enhance your erogenous zones: It sounds like fun. The third is this quiet and aloof bisexual guy, phony sweet, with short blond curls and the air of a sulky boy. He complains that everyone wants to fuck him because he's so cute. He wants to grow old and get ugly so that people will "love me for who I am." I think he works in a boutique but I'm not sure.

"When you're old and ugly," I say, "no one's going to give a shit about you."

I shouldn't have ragged on him like that; maybe I was too harsh. But I don't really care. I've had enough of these people who constantly blabber about themselves. These three are totally unimportant. They're silly and annoying. They serve my purposes only on Saturday so that I won't die of boredom on the train, which goes so slowly in the darkness, without any fucking thing to look at outside but the stream of lights along the tracks that flash by and hypnotize you like an optical illusion.

The name of the club is Amnesia.

Only a few years ago, when I was a little girl, I lived around here; I mean, I was born here. I came into the world the same day that Amnesia opened, in September, Virgo with Gemini in the ascendant. My house was right near the huge billboard for the new dance club, at Exit 17 on the state highway—it was a huge, bluish-white flying saucer that seemed to hover in a halo of milky haze in the middle of the road, between the silhouettes of two hills like the ones in *Close Encounters of the Third Kind*.

Many people that night thought they saw a UFO. When I get totally jazzed and I really want to blow people away, I tell them that I was born on the night the Earth was invaded by Martians, under the sign of the virgin alien.

I come into the club. I'm already pumped up in that good way, excited and happy (I crack up when I think that it wasn't the stork that brought me but a spaceship). It feels like the bow of my ship is parting a liquid wall of music, light, aphrodisiac smells, and the radioactivity of scattered longings and desires.

They promise you everything, and everything seems possible. I'm looking for my ecstasy. The kind I like.

My ecstasy tab is pink, with the shape of an elephant's head stamped into it. It reminds me of Dumbo: Flying on ecstasy is strange and funny, the way that little elephant with the big ears was. It's an impossible flight. It makes you want to cry and laugh; it's weird at the beginning, then seems natural and almost real, like when you dream you have wings, and you wish you could live that trip every single day of your life.

This is what the drug does (though it isn't right to call something a drug that makes you feel normal while normally you don't): It lets you feel *right*. All the people around you are a shitty bunch of assholes. When you first meet them, they seem excellent; then when you get to know them, you're totally bummed out because they are so stupid, egotistical, and empty. Ecstasy lets you see them the way they should be: always marvelous. It modifies all the bullshit they say by making your brain send out some substance that changes your perceptions, improves them. It lets you live the kind of life you don't have, the right kind; it lets you talk to angels.

And having sex on ecstasy is awesome. It's like a 3D porno film of whatever you want, a nebulization of sensations that bathes you, exciting every part of your body. It's not only about a cock and a cunt rubbing and banging together; it's much more. It's like coming out of the shower with tiny, warm droplets covering your skin, your hair, your shoulders, your nipples, clinging around your belly button, to your pubic hair, your lips, your eyelids. Your whole body is an organ of pleasure. You are fucked right down to your soul. You are like an enormous heart that receives boiling lymph, and the pumping, the boom-boom of percussion instruments bursts open your chest, kicking you in the uterus over and over. Others are outside and inside of you at the same time. All differences fall away, all isolation. You love everyone and everyone loves you. The thousand dancing bodies around you could be just one, and you immerse yourself in them as if in a sea—shouts, leaps, turns, whirls, dances with the cunt (didn't some famous dancer call them that, who was it?). In your dance you unlock all of the energy you have down there, love and pain, rage and longing, betrayed hopes and dreams of happiness. You can do everything with the cunt—destroy and save, kill and heal.

It is clean and healthy, the sex from ecstasy: You don't risk AIDS, nothing happens that you don't want to, people are like images, and you are in the hands of a divine creature who loves you, knows and understands you, and is as able to dry your tears as he is to make you come by licking your clit.

And in the exaltation of all this movement at 120 decibels, in the insane vortex of colors, of arms and legs seemingly detached from bodies being shot out of amplifiers, all is motionless. Or at least I perceive it as at rest, calm and pure, like one of those funerary sculptures of dead little boys on which women bestow kisses, a good *Dylan Dog* story—a world that is dead and at peace, full of defunct myths (Jim Morrison will never again be able to delude you, where he is now) and of beautiful, young corpses on top of me, under me, like the marble of a tomb.

He suddenly appears before me: He is beautiful like a solar eclipse. I say eclipse because, in orbit around the dance floor, he passes in front of the mirrored ball and blocks it out; I can only see his black form outlined in a twilight of thumping music.

Tall, sinuous, long electric-blond hair, he is wearing shiny spandex pants and a white T-shirt with Kurt Cobain's face printed on it. He has a rock star's face, its features animal-like but delicate, sensual, the skin taut and unreal looking, covered with white pancake makeup. He is a fabulous erotic clown, possesses beauty surpassing the beauty that I fantasize and project outside of myself.

We look at each other, and a spark of interest passes between us. We begin to dance for each other, each of us displaying ourselves in movement so as to attract the other. Our sides lightly brush, our long hair flying. As we approach each other, our dance becomes more personal and intimate, more engaged.

We smile at each other.

"Hi!" I shout, my voice unable to rise above the volume of the music.

"Hi!"

"What's your name?"

We shout our names (I can't understand his) and our ages at each other: he is twenty-two, I'm eighteen.

"I'm an alien! I came down to earth in a spaceship," I joke.

"What?"

He doesn't understand, but it doesn't matter.

From his appearance, my shadowy blond boy is everything I've been looking for: He is perfect, as long as he doesn't talk. I imagine his tenderness and his courage, his sense of humor and his generosity, and I know that he will be different from the usual guys who take you for a fool, and that he will love me forever, "you at least in the universe," like in the Mia Martini song. As long as he doesn't ruin everything by opening his mouth and beginning to talk bullshit. You could love the whole world, if it would only stay silent.

The boy makes a gesture with his hand, waving me over to the bar. I follow him, and we still haven't touched each other physically, even if in our heads we are already more than close. We've sniffed, licked, clung to each other, and screwed to the point of exhaustion. Providing that he doesn't start talking and telling me who he is and what he does. And yet, god damn, he starts telling me that he is an initiate of I don't know what church of Satan, obviously to make himself seem more interesting. "Nothing to do, you understand, with those maniacs that dig up cemeteries and pour blood on themselves. Ours is a responsible choice of beliefs."

Another satanist, the usual head case. Why do people always try to make themselves so interesting? He's a boring jerk like the others. For a little while, I enjoyed thinking that he was a mix between Arthur Rimbaud the blue prince and the vampire Lestat. But why can't you ever find someone who is not a put-on, someone who is special, really special?

I'm no longer listening to him. I'm looking at the dead face of Kurt Cobain. (I don't find his suicide at all incomprehensible; I think it's *excellent* that he told everyone to go to hell when he had albums in the Top Ten and was up to his ass in success.) I look at the living face of this guy what's-his-name, with his lips moving, and I'm thinking, "Be quiet, be quiet, be quiet." I drag him into the club's sumptuous bathroom, full of pink velvet and hot babes who eat him alive with their eyes. They stare at me, burning with envy. There's a short guy with a dark, badly trimmed beard and little round glasses who is talking on a cell phone.

We go into the last stall and close the door.

He stretches his arms out in an ironic gesture of surrender, as if he were giving in to me. I lower his tights, revealing a penis that is pinkish like a rosebud, very graceful, with a little glans suffocated in folds of flesh. I play with this sleepy organ a little while. I tickle it, tantalize it, grasp it, caress it. It doesn't get erect, and I'm not able to slip my favorite condom on it— ultrathin violet-colored with ribbing—if it's not hard. I could try to take it in my mouth, but then all of those horrible images from anti-AIDS commercials come to mind, with all those infected people giving off a green flow like the Hulk. How can I be sure that he didn't get the virus from some woman who got it from her husband who got it from a hooker who got it from her client who got it from a bisexual guy who got it from some woman who got it from a drug addict?

Then I say, what the fuck, you'll never do anything if you're always thinking about AIDS, and I begin to lick his balls. I tease him with my tongue, I suck him between my lips, I taste the flavor of his sweet albumen: still nothing. Soft and salivated, it slips right out of me.

Maybe it's because of the alcohol and the pills.

Now he stops me, respectfully, and he assumes control of the game.

He makes me sit down on the toilet and spread my legs. He takes the zipper on my skirt and unzips it from the hem to the waistline (a thing that always excites me—it makes me feel like someone is opening my body all the way from the bottom to the top). Then he lowers my panties, rolling them over my thigh-high stockings down to my ankles, and bares my breast. I sit like that, like a doll, less than dressed, more than naked. He begins to softly run his member along my neck, through my hair, in a gentle, patient caress. Then it descends to my chest, where I hold it for a moment, squeezing it between my breasts, pressing it against my belly in slow circular motions. His thrusting against me becomes more urgent, more ardent, but he does not yet have an erection.

He trembles slightly, tenses, breathes heavily; so concentrated, so closed within himself and within his unappeasable desire, that he is like a dead person, or someone about to faint. He is trying to satisfy himself mentally. Perhaps he is using the friction between his absent erection and my flesh to wear down to and expose another organ, one buried within the gray matter of his brain.

I feel sympathy and gratitude for this odd boy who, without abusing me, delights me by involving me in his imagination.

He kneels between my legs, presses his mouth to my labia (he too could care less about AIDS), and penetrates my cunt with his tongue. God, he has something right on the tip of it: a stud, a tiny, pointed metal thing. He plunges it in, pulls it out, presses it against my clit, then begins again, over and over. It's great, it's to die for, this cyborg sex. Outside, the short guy's cell phone has not quit ringing for a second (it can't be that so many people are calling him because they care, so he must be dealing). I associate that annoying *ring-ring-ring* with the orgasm that explodes in my head, with that metal prosthesis rhythmically stroking inside of me. I lose consciousness of everything around me; or rather, I suddenly come before being able to regain consciousness.

He stands up and rests his inert cock against my belly, leaving two fingers inside me and moving them slowly so that my orgasm diminishes gradually, like the sound of an echo or the circular ripples from a stone tossed into water. He murmurs, sighs, is traversed by shivers. Perhaps he comes too, somehow, by reflection, by absorbing my physical sensations and converting them into a curious moral pleasure.

"Shall we go?"

We leave the disco in the dust. I have taken another tab, and he too is "ecstatic." We feel this incredible sense of well-being coming upon us. We hold hands, intertwining our fingers, and remain welded through them.

I don't know what neighborhood I'm in (oh shit, I've forgotten everything, except that I know how to read and write!). I'm walking around in some small piece of hinterland that could be located anyplace on the planet between America and the third world.

I look around me: Over there is a parking structure, over here a gas station with a tanker truck filling up the pumps, straight ahead the Coop with a neon sign (an "o" is burned out, so it reads *Cop*), and behind a Chinese restaurant that is closing. A skinny Chinese man, with his bones sticking out all over from hard work, his face drawn and tired, is dumping a bucket of water and rotten cabbages in a barrel. I raise my eyes and read the electronic board indicating the temperature, twenty-seven degrees centigrade: Twenty-seven degrees, this much at least makes sense, you know that it must be hot.

It's insane: I don't know where I am, really.

I'm not afraid or worried. A diabolical hilarity instead sweeps over me, like I used to feel a few years ago with my girlfriends from school when we would just laugh like idiots for no reason at all. I'm having fun, like when I go into sex shops. The fake cocks and cunts put me in a good mood, like the toothless smiles of nursing infants do. You go into these stores containing all the things people want without knowing how to admit it, and you finally see it all laid out in one place in a shameless, endearing orgy of objects, and you leave thanking heaven you have nothing to hide, feeling better and freer.

We go down into an underground walkway, still holding hands, and we act like idiots a little. I shout and run, dragging him along behind me. I climb onto his back to ride him like a horse, and he lifts me up and spins me around. I laugh like a witch on a bright spring night. It stinks of piss. It seems like half the people in the world have urinated in here. The ivory-colored tiles are streaked with dried yellowish-orange filaments. The odor mixes with the generic smell of the city: preserved foods, carbonic acid, smoke, sewers, gasoline, and I think I like it that way. I don't know how to express this very well, but this piss left here and there wherever it falls is rightful. It's nasty, but nasty in a rightful way, not like the endless sickening bullshit that people always talk, and all their fine feelings. This is my world, I love it, and in all my melancholy I'm at home here.

"My car is nearby. I'll take you home."

I double over from laughing so hard. I don't know where my home is, I tell him in one ear, sticking my tongue inside it.

"So we'll go to my house."

We climb into his car (a long silvery thing that looks like it could break the sound barrier). We take off, driving fast. I rest my hand on his thigh, the one and only place it should be right now.

He tells me that he has his own apartment, has money, works in his father's store. They install televisions, satellite dishes, etcetera—boring stuff like that. I turn on the radio and lean back against the headrest, rocking my head to the music. I push my hand even deeper between his legs.

We go faster and faster in the heavy, humid night.

The headlights lash the dark ribbon of road. I slip out of my panties and skirt. I work my hand under the fabric of his pants and touch his silky, soft cock.

It must be gorgeous erect, long and large, white like his painted face.

He quivers, but it doesn't get hard. Fine with me.

I realize that I'm dying with desire to feel his impotent cock against my clit and the opening of my vagina (penetration is only one way to come, like any other). What I want from him, right now, is his sweet cock to fuck and to swallow, to make my own.

"Stop the car as soon as you can," I whisper to him.

There was a curve, and he didn't see it, distracted perhaps by my fingers: we're flying, almost hanging in midair, like those dancers that give the impression of being able to suspend themselves for an instant at the top of a jump. My heart skips a beat; I have no time to think.

Then down.

A violent impact slams us from one side to the other. The seatbelt snaps me backward like a slingshot in reverse.

The tires are skidding totally without traction. It is a sensation that reaches me directly through the wheels, horrible and riveting. I scream like on a roller coaster at the amusement park. A vertiginous sliding, a collision that prolongs itself in other collisions, a chain of them, the sound of glass shattering, the seatbelt still restraining me.

We come to a stop against something: a wall, a high-tension fence? No, it's a billboard with an ass on it, an enormous ass illuminated by one of our headlights (the other must be broken) suspended above us like a full moon.

We ran off the road, what fun.

I detach the seatbelt and stretch myself carefully. It doesn't seem possible that I'm really unhurt. A little suffocated giggle comes out of me—the fear too turns out to be nothing but a big joke.

I turn toward the boy. He is lying on his back on the car seat, which has collapsed backward. He moans.

"What's wrong?"

He moves his pupils slowly. His lips form a silent, incomprehensible word. Then a beaming smile, as if he's achieved something, spreads across his face. He was only playing: He doesn't have a scratch on him either.

We are alone in the compartment of the car, in the suburban desert, like the nonexistent astronauts from the phony spaceship that landed on the day I was born.

No one to check up on us, no rules to follow, no normality, just the ecstasy.

I climb on top of him and undress him, grabbing at and yanking the printed face of Kurt Cobain. He has a body that looks like it's made of milk, voluptuous, with tiny nipples that you'd like to bite and make bleed. I kiss his upturned and astonished eyes, the half-open mouth that reminds me of that of a praying saint. As a little girl, not many years ago, the little statues of saints and Christs would excite me, their beautiful wax faces seized by agony as if in an erotic passion; their open hands the hands of sleepers, their fingers like sea anemones, their bodies enraptured, pervaded by aching sweetness as they swoon. I've always confused ecstasy with something missing, with losing one's senses. During the long summer afternoons, I used to pretend to faint and would throw myself on the bed. The idea of falling in a faint provoked a kind of agonizing languor in me that made me twist and turn in restless desire on the sheets, already impregnated with my smells. I felt totally erotic, from head to toe, but would deny myself an orgasm. I didn't touch myself because I wanted to remain full of that swooning sexuality, feel it swelling inside of me until I could no longer bear it. I breathed deeply, lying prone and motionless, waiting for the excitement to drain away, not down out of my clitoris, but through my whole being, in a vaporous haze mixed with the accompanying shadows of the room.

I am on top of him, grinding myself against his delicious, defenseless, and vulnerable body. I rub my erect clit along him, feeling shocks of stimulation shooting through it. I dance lightly upon him, caress him with my sex; I redraw him, tracing out the mental map of my desires. I don't know what I am doing, but I know it is beautiful, perfect, the thing that I need. I am fucking and flying in ecstasy; I am screwing all the gods of rock, dead and ascended to heaven. I love my black angel—I am raping every part of him with my hands and my cunt, leaving sticky loving moisture on his thighs, his belly, his hips. His face shines in tenebrous pallor. I bury my fingers in his blond hair, I cover him like a sea, I catch up his tender penis in the cavity of my sex. It is like taking a child; it makes me feel almost sad. Maybe I will return to the time I was a child, when I was bounced on my grandfather's knee, when I loved Dumbo, when I still felt loved and protected, swaddled in the world's affection. I cover him with kisses and cry, the tenderness I feel is killing me. I feel almost as if I had an oyster between my labia, a soft sea creature that I could devour. I contract the muscles of my vagina, unexpectedly stirring new sensations. I relax, and I bathe him once again.

He is shaken by a brief convulsion. A thin line of blood is drying on his temple (didn't he come out of the accident unscathed?). He must have hit his head against the windshield in the spot where it is cracked in a spiderweb of radiating lines.

I take my head in my hands and lean my face close to his. A little tremor, then a kind of yielding, and he exhales into my mouth. It's not possible that he is really doing this, it must be a joke. He can't be dead—it can't be that I inhaled his death while embracing him....

I can't believe it's true. But if I believed it, it would be the highest and most overpowering erotic emotion I've ever felt.

I decide to shrug off believing or not believing. It is what it is.

I then obliterate myself in a powerful orgasm.

It is too much. I scream because I want to keep him with me so that it can never end. I come furiously. I feel like my brain catches fire and burns. I die with my boy.

It is the flight of the elephant (from the alien spaceship on which I arrived from outer space), a night that is "different, but truly different," like in the song by Ron.

The perfect night that I've always invoked.

The night of my first and only love.

# Speedball
## *Cara Bruce*

I slide the needle in and out, desperately seeking a vein. I pull out of the spot I am in and clench my fist over and over. I do push-ups, jumping jacks, getting myself in shape for the sole purpose of getting a fix. I sit back down and tie off again, tightly clenching my fist. The syringe is loaded and ready to go. I smack my arm until finally I see a slight tinge of blue. A vein! I push the needle in and draw back, watching as the hit registers and the red blood begins to mix with the black tar and invisible cocaine. I pull in and push out, the needle making love with my arm, and then I push the plunger in, emptying all of the contents into my bloodstream, pull it out for the final time, and untie my arm. I hit orgasm—or the junkie's version of orgasm: a rush of warmth as the coke slams me against that great glass ceiling of being high, and a rush of calm as the heroin floods my muscles, my joints, all of my body.

I jump up with the rush of the coke, wild-eyed and hyper-aware. I feel full of love. It is way different than when I simply do heroin. Nowadays, doing just heroin doesn't make me feel any different than doing anything else—it just makes me not sick. My addiction has made me boring and has stolen my libido. I haven't had sex in months and have no desire to. But suddenly, with the surge of cocaine, my boyfriend is actually starting to look desirable—a sure sign I am fucked up, because he has gotten so strung-out that he probably doesn't look desirable to anything.

So there he is, tying off and beginning his search for the ultimate high, or the ultimate wellness, and here am I, horny for the first time in months. Granted, it's a narco-enraged type of horniness, a complete drug-induced libido enhancement, but I don't care. It's a feeling other than what I had been feeling for these days/months/years on and off and on and on and on again. And it's a good one.

He hits himself and looks up. I can tell he's feeling the rush—that initial flood that all is right in this world, that superhuman feeling that nothing can stop him. He runs to the bathroom and turns on all the water faucets. He claims this intensifies the ringing in his ears, and he enjoys that. It's a sad day when you listen to the sink for fun.

But after he's done he still looks good, I ask him if he feels OK. He does. I sidle toward him, suggesting that we both take a shower. I rub my hands up his body; we're both sweating from the toxic waste combo we've recently injected. I rub my hands up and over his bony frame, lightly fingering the scars of abscesses and other things that go bump when you miss.

He looks at me oddly. I am definitely the strange one here, the one who is suddenly doing something so totally different and radical that it is freaking him out. I'm instigating some kind of drugged-up foreplay. But I barely remember the art of seduction. I barely remember anything beyond who I am or how good coke feels. And it *is* good coke—good enough to overpower the waves of heroin that keep creeping up around me like smoke ringlets that innocuously fill up a room until you die. But that's the best part about a speedball. You don't get the coke crash; the heroin catches your fall.

But enough about drugs, let's talk about sex. Because right now, sex is the only thing I want. I feel like I am in the middle of a dope kick when masturbating is the only thing that can release tension. During a kick, my libido rushes at me like a speeding car, careening out of control as if the man driving it has just had a heart attack and his foot is stuck on the pedal—an unstoppable condition. I could masturbate ten times a day and still need more. During a kick I can come quickly, but I am hard-pressed to get enough.

Lee looks at me again as I kind of ooze around him. He looks different; it takes me more than a few minutes to realize it's the fact that his pupils are more than mere pinpricks. I think back to how I read somewhere, once, that women used to put belladonna in their eyes to dilate their pupils and make them more attractive. I'm not sure if it's the pupil thing, but he does look better—or at least human.

So he finally gets the hint and takes my hand and leads me toward the bathroom. We undress quickly. Too stoned for foreplay, we turn the water to scalding and let steam fill up the bathroom. I am eager to feel the water on my now-stinky drug-addict body, and I let it run over me. Lee still looks hesitant, as if water is some evil entity that he does not agree with. We both cram into the shower, huddling together, neither of us wanting to be in that cold space where the water doesn't reach. We kiss, our tongues moving in and out of each other's mouths like the snakes we have become.

My hand moves down his body and finds his cock. It is limp. I don't know what I was expecting—that the coke would overpower his physical functions the way it had over-powered my libido? I continue trying for a few minutes, my coke-induced brain hoping to resurrect his dope-filled dick.

"It still feels good," he says, although we are very much aware that penetration by his dick is not going to happen. I don't really care much about using his dick at this point: I care more about just getting off. I turn off the water and we get out of the shower.

Draped only in a towel I lead him down the hall to the bedroom and drag him to the room that currently functions as a living room/office. I push him down on the bed. He looks excited, though both of us know that nothing is going to happen for him. I dig through my underwear drawer, looking for my vibrator.

"You can watch," I say playfully. He strokes his dick and curses the fact that it won't work.

I grab my favorite vibrator and straddle him. He's still attempting to get something out of his cock. His eyes are wide with the promise of a show. I turn the vibrator on and hand it to him, while with my own fingers I flick my clit. It's been so long since I masturbated—but it's just like riding a bike; quickly I pick up the pace. With my other hand I move his toward me. He jerks out of a drowsy nod and inserts the toy into my cunt. He moves it in and out, as I rock back and forth on him. With one hand he's fucking me with my toy, with the other he's massaging his dick in an absolute frenzy, trying desperately to make it work.

At this point I could care less about him. Then again, I'm a drug addict, so in general I could care less about most things. I continue working my clit until my juices finally begin to flow. I wonder if I can actually come, though at this point I don't even care, because it feels so good.

"Faster," I moan, and he moves beneath me. I am vaguely aware that he is achieving a hard-on. I shut my eyes and throw my head back, feeling incredibly sexy masturbating in front of him.

Even through his stupor, he picks up on this. "You look so hot," he whispers. "I love to watch you play with yourself."

I go for it. The show is for both of us, and I'm not stopping until I achieve some sort of release. When he pulls out the vibrator I moan at the aching emptiness. His dick moves against my leg; I reach down to help guide it in. I am soaked with juices. I pull him into me. He feels so good, filling me up and beginning a slow, methodical stroke. I keep at my finger work and let the drugs flowing through my body enhance every sensation. I had forgotten what it feels like to have sex on a speedball. It's fantastic.

"You feel so fucking good," I groan. He moves faster, in and out, in and out. I close my eyes again and imagine his dick as a needle moving in and out of my arm, waiting for that ultimate pleasure of the release. I am tweaked out, on edge, and it begins to seem urgent that I have an orgasm. I need this. My fingers are in a fucking frenzy.

"Harder," I scream, my hand pushing down on his head. He complies, fucking me as hard as he can. I haven't been fucked like this for months. It feels just as good as getting high. The pressure inside me is building. I tighten my thighs, increasing my speed on his dick as well as with my fingers.

Suddenly I feel it rising through me: my first orgasm in months, heightened by the sensation of the drugs. It crashes through me in waves, mimicking the effect of the speed/heroin combo. I scream, falling forward onto him, my body wracking as if I'm having a withdrawal seizure.

I lie for a minute on top of him. "Do you think you can come?" I whisper, vaguely aware that he is still inside me, though I can feel him going flaccid.

"I don't think so," he says, "but that felt good."

I roll over and we lie panting for a minute, sticky and reeling.

He gets up after a few seconds and moves to the dresser where he pulls out our drugs and rig.

"So," he says, as if we had just been sitting around watching TV. "Do you want to get high?"

# The Amy Special
*Lisa Wolfe*

.

What she remembers most is the silky feeling of sliding down his chocolatey body and the distinct sensation of his tightly coiled hair, wiry against her face.

"I like your pubic hair."

"Well, that's a first."

"The way it's so crinkly." Like brand-new steel wool, she thinks.

"Courtesy of Africa," Michael says.

So she's sliding down and she smells him, clean and musky and—no it's not just a cliché, the chocolate, he actually smells like chocolate, from the cocoa butter lotion he uses on his skin. And when she kisses him on the mouth, she smells the cocoa laced with the cool scent of the mints he perpetually sucks on.

"You're my long, tall chocolate mint," she says as she slides down again, first licking, and then slowly draping her mouth over him.

The amazing thing was, ordinarily she didn't love dicks. Not *really*.

"You know," she told him once, as they were driving down the coast, "it's not like I *love* dicks. That's why it's so special that I love *your* dick—yours—it's personal. I don't *need* a dick to come—I like tongues and fingers better."

"I know," he said, raising his eyebrows, with that slow, quiet grin.

But in truth, she thinks to herself, watching him drive, his long fingers resting lightly on the wheel—she *likes* dicks. She likes them inside her, pumping away hard and deep like there's no tomorrow, or pressing against her thigh, or outlined under the fabric of blue jeans, or sliding into her delicately like a hot whisper. She just doesn't feel...worshipful—something like that. Should she? Are there women out there in the real world who say, "Please, baby, let me suck you"? Who don't get sore jaws and lips, or don't even notice, because they're so turned on? Does she in fact have a double standard, wanting a man who worships at the altar of the divine yoni, yet not worshipping his (what was it called?) lingam. She looked over at him driving, at his profile, and then down at his crotch. He caught her looking and they laughed.

So anyway, there she is, sucking away on him, and she looks up for a moment, and—this is it, this is what she remembers most about him—she sees him watching her, his eyes dark and hot and liquid, and this turns her on more than anything, him looking at her sucking and her looking at him looking at her, it goes direct to her clit and then up to her nipples and back down again. After the first time this happened, every time she sucked him she would always look at him to watch him watching her, even though it strained her neck, and she would watch for a time until she went back to her handiwork. And as she teased her tongue down the shaft and then slowly back up to the head, he would moan, and then she would put her whole mouth on him, making sure not to bite him, sucking on him just like Amy.

It was her ex-husband who told her about Amy, the tooth-less old Vietnamese woman who gave the best head in Da Nang. Amy was renowned among American soldiers, who came to her for, well, succor. When he first told her about Amy, she was pissed. Were our tax dollars paying for this? Sexual and racial imperialism, colonial exploitation of women, and so forth. But Amy intrigued her. Who was this woman—a victim of political exploitation, or an accomplished businesswoman? Did Amy turn the loss of her teeth into a boon, taking the secret pain and polishing it, using it, until it became something beautiful, the basis for her famous craft and art? So her ex-husband taught her how to do him just like Amy, as if she were toothless, unarmed, a gummy mistress who gives the ultimate, bite-free blowjob. She learned to pull her upper lip over her top teeth and her lower lip over the bottom ones, so that as she sucked, she felt like a toothless wonder, and her lip muscles grew strong and resilient.

So she's giving Michael the Amy Special, and he's happily moaning, and then he inevitably says, "I want to eat you."

So what does she do? She doesn't argue with him, she slides up and kisses him on the mouth and falls off to the side, languorously, because languor suits her. And he starts kissing her thighs but she moves him up to her nipples and says, "Start high," and he practices his magic on her nipples with his tongue, pulling and rolling and sucking and flicking. Then he gradually moves south, stopping for nips here and there, down to her belly and her panties. He slides his tongue under the elastic and all around the edges, moving down to the apex and *flick-flick,* he teases her at the edges of the crotch of her panties. She is fairly soaked now, waiting, impatient, but enjoying the torture. She doesn't want to beg, but she wants him to get on with the show. She starts to moan, and then— this is what she remembers most about him—he traces his fingers along the edges of her panties as if he's finger-painting in slow motion, and hooks his fingers under the elastic right next to her pussy and slowly pulls them down. At this point she stops breathing. She knows breathing is a good thing but she stops anyway while she waits. Then he picks up the nipple action again, but now with his fingers, twisting and pulling and pinching, and her breath comes out in pants and plaintive sounds, mewling sounds that she would stop if she could but she can't so she waits while he licks around the edges of her hair and labia until he gets closer and closer and laps one side of her pussy, and then the other. She lets out a sigh of relief from deep in her throat, which is short-lived because then she is on the next rise of terror and pleasure, as he starts in with the slow circles. The circles trace around her clit but don't quite reach it, which is torture and of course she could take his head and move it but at this point she has given up control, hoping that he will really take her there, won't he?, that she won't be abandoned at the crest or just before it, that it really will happen and just as she is fighting this last shred of control, he moves his tongue over to her clit and she lets out a guttural sound of affirmation, and then they are on the home stretch, and he goes slower and slower, which gets her closer and closer until she is so close that if he would only go a little faster she would go over the edge but he knows and she knows that if he goes too fast she will never come at all so he keeps going slower until she wants to pound him, but she waits because she knows that he knows what he is doing and finally it does hover and break, and she is screaming even though she has promised herself to try not to make so much noise, it could wake the neighbors, it's too much, she's too much, she's embarrassed even, but then it doesn't matter after all, it just comes out of her like a righteous wail, and she comes like a long fountain, one of those luxurious comes that starts locally and spreads to her womb and toes and mind and she confirms this with a soft sigh of relief.

And then it is quiet. Almost. Because now he is putting on a condom and sliding himself in, wasting no time, and he is making those extended animal sounds and saying things like, "I'm going to pump you so good, do you want me to?" and she is whispering "yes, yes, yes" like Molly Bloom, and he is filling her up, it feels like coming home, they are both coming home, and this brings on a different kind of come now, a ripping, longing love sort of come, a don't-ever-leave-me kind of come, a you-belong-to-me-don't-ever-fuck-anyone-else kind of come. And she's looking into his beautiful dark eyes and she says, "I feel it—I feel it in my heart." She doesn't know why she's saying this, but it's as if her cunt and womb had moved up into her heart, no longer relegated to their functional geography, and he says, "I want you to—I want you to feel it in your heart." And then she's having another one of those bonus orgasms riding the tail-end of the last one, a ripple effect, and then he comes too, thrashing and moaning, and then they are lying there, sweaty and proud of themselves, and breathing hard into the silence, and that familiar feeling comes creeping over her, she can't help it, the habit of it, and she thinks *What will I remember most about him?*

# About the Authors

**KIM ADDONIZIO** lives in San Francisco and teaches writing in the Bay Area. She is the author of three collections of poetry: *The Philosopher's Club*, *Jimmy and Rita*, and *Tell Me*, which was a finalist for the National Book Award. She also coauthored, with Dorianne Laux, *The Poet's Companion: A Guide to the Pleasures of Writing Poetry* (W. W. Norton). Her work has received several awards, including two NEA Fellowships, and has appeared in numerous zines, literary journals, and anthologies.

**LISA ARCHER** lives in San Francisco. Her work appears in *Best Bisexual Women's Erotica*, the *San Francisco Bay Guardian*, and a variety of other publications.

**KATE BACHUS'S** fiction has appeared in *SkinTwo*'s webzine and magazine. She has a lovely wife and son, and counts search and rescue, firefighting, and BDSM among her interests. Visit her website: http://soiuser.hyperchat.com/maenad/kate.html

**CHEYENNE BLUE** writes travel guides and erotica, using her surroundings as inspiration for both. She lives in the United States, but thinks of the world as a big place full of borders to be crossed.

**TALIA BRAHM** is the alter ego of a mild-mannered government records clerk. She has sold enough of her writing to whet her appetite, but not enough to feed herself on a regular basis. She plans one day to shed her bureaucratic cocoon and emerge as her true literary self. Until then, you've got something to think about while you're waiting in line at the DMV.

**CARA BRUCE** is the editor of VenusOrVixen.com and Venus or Vixen Press. She edited *Viscera* and the upcoming collections *Best Bisexual Women's Erotica* and *Obsessed: Fetish Erotica*. Her erotic writing has been published in numerous anthologies, including *Best American Erotica 2001, Best Women's Erotica 2001 and 2000, Best Lesbian Erotica 2000, Mammoth Best Erotica of the Year, Starf\*cker*, and many more.

**DIANA EVE CAPLAN** has published under various names in *Best Lesbian Erotica 2000, Dykes with Baggage: Lesbians and the Lighter Side of Therapy,* and *Uniform Sex*. She is writing a screenplay and editing an anthology by and for lesbian and gay step-parents.

**ISABELLE CARRUTHERS** lives and writes in New Orleans. Her fiction has been published in *Prometheus, Philogyny: Girls Who Kiss and Tell,* and *Mammoth's Best Erotica,* and has appeared in various Internet magazines including *Zoetrope All-Story Extra, Amatory Ink,* and *MindKites*. She serves as fiction editor for two popular erotica webzines, Clean Sheets and Mind Caviar.

**RENEE CARTER HALL** has published speculative erotica online at Clean Sheets and in the forthcoming *Matriarch's Way*. Although most of her fiction involves other worlds or fantastic happenings, she leads a fairly normal life with her husband in Virginia.

**RAPHAELA CROWN** lives in Jerusalem. Her erotic writing can be found in *Bedroom Eyes: Stories of Lesbians in the Boudoir* and online at Clean Sheets; her other work has appeared in a wide variety of publications, including *The Paris Review*, *The New Republic*, *The Massachusetts Review*, *Seventeen* magazine, and *The University of Pennsylvania Law Review*.

**KATE DOMINIC**, a Los Angeles–based freelance writer, is the author of *Any 2 People, Kissing* (Down There Press). Her erotic stories also appear in *Herotica 6 and 7, Best Lesbian Erotica 2000, Best Women's Erotica 2000 and 2001, Lip Service, Wicked Words I and IV, Strange Bedfellows,* and many other anthologies and magazines.

**SACCHI GREEN** leads multiple lives in western Massachusetts, the mountains of New Hampshire, and her libidinous imagination. Some of the fantasies she's wrestled into story form can be read in *Best Women's Erotica 2001;* the 1999, 2000, and 2001 editions of *Best Lesbian Erotica;* and the anthologies *Set in Stone, Zaftig: Well-Rounded Erotica*, and *More Technosex.*

**ELSPETH POTTER** lives in Philadelphia. Her erotic fiction appearsin *Best Lesbian Erotica 2001*. She sent "Twisted Beauty" to *BWE 2002* without showing it to anyone first.

**SUSANNAH INDIGO** is editor of cleansheets.com. Her work has appeared in numerous anthologies, including *Best American Erotica, Best Women's Erotica*, and the *Herotica* series.

**A. R. MORLAN'S** work has appeared in over 100 magazines, anthologies, and websites, including *Love in Vein: Stories of Erotic Vampirism, Prisoners of the Night, Cherished Blood*, and other erotic, science fiction, and horror publications.

**KATHERINE LOVE** has been published online at Clean Sheets and in *Best Women's Erotica 2000*. She lives in Minneapolis.

**CLAUDIA SALVATORI** has published erotic fiction in *In the Forbidden City: An Anthology of Erotic Fiction by Italian Women*.

**HELEN SETTIMANA** is a clay artist, teacher, and writer of erotica who lives in Toronto. She grew up in a family tradition rich with tales of Canadian military life. Her stories and poetry have appeared in *Best Women's Erotica 2001,* in *Prometheus*, and in various "literotica" Web publications, including The Erotica Readers' Association, Clean Sheets, and Scarlet Letters.

**SUSAN ST. AUBIN** is a mild-mannered administrative coordinator by day and a racy pornographer at night. Her work has appeared in diverse journals and anthologies, including *The Reed, Short Story Review, Yellow Silk, Libido*, the *Herotica* series, *Best American Erotica, Best Lesbian Erotica*, and online at Clean Sheets.

**ANNE TOURNEY'S** erotic fiction has appeared in various publications, including *Best American Erotica* and *Best Women's Erotica*, the anthologies *Zaftig: Well-Rounded Erotica* and *The Unmade Bed*, and the online magazines Scarlet Letters and Clean Sheets. She has published horror and dark fantasy in *Embraces: Dark Erotica* and *Dark Regions*.

**ALISON TYLER** is the author of sixteen naughty novels, most recently *Learning to Love It* and *Strictly Confidential*, both published by Black Lace. Look for her seductive short stories in anthologies, including *Erotic Travel Tales* (Cleis Press), *Noirotica 3* and *4* (Black Books), and *Wicked Words 4* and *5* (Black Lace).

**LISA WOLFE** is the pen name of a woman who lives in the San Francisco Bay Area. Her plays and performance pieces have been seen on the stage, but this is her first time in print. Writing erotica is the most fun she's ever had with a laptop. She extends thanks Lori Habige.

# About the Editor

**MARCY SHEINER** is editor of the *Best Women's Erotica* series and *The Oy of Sex: Jewish Women's Erotica* (Cleis Press). She is also editor of *Herotica 4, 5, 6,* and *7* (Plume; Down There Press). Her stories and essays have appeared in many anthologies and publications. She is the author of *Sex for the Clueless* (Kensington Press). Her website is www.marcysheiner.tripod.com.